His
Eyes
Are
Watching

Book two in the 'I Am My Sister's Keeper' series

Author Kilene *'Ki'* Williams

1

Book cover photography:
Jeff Deshommes and *Ferline Jeune*
Dez'Noir Elite Photography

Book cover photoshoot creative direction:
Brittney Nugent

Book Cover Models:
Dez'Noir Models:
Brittney Nugent (as Victoria) and
Nicole Perez (as Sade)

Acknowledgements

To my village, you know without hesitation exactly who you are. I thank you from the depths of my soul. I love you, and there is absolutely nothing you can do about it!

To my 'Irish Twin', my favorite male singer, songwriter and poet, Mr. Leo, I love you. I thank you big brother for being the first person to encourage me to finally start sharing my writing with the world. Thank you for having my back. I know your eyes are always watching, and your little sis appreciates it.

To the readers, thank you all for your time and support. *You hold the match that strikes. Let no one dim your light.*

His
Eyes
Are
Watching

Chapter One

Still Eyes See

TJ

Known to many as a fierce, yet respectful businessman, my father hid his alter ego from society. His closest friends had no idea who he really was. There was a dark side that only arrived when he was at home. I was his stress reliever. He tortured, sodomized, raped, beat and during his worst spells, chained me to a pole in the basement. Sometimes I would go hours without food and water.

We didn't keep company. One thing my father never allowed were outside spirits entering the threshold of his home. Any entertaining he and my mother did was always outside of the home. After my mother's death, I knew it was a way to keep me isolated from the outside world. No one could be privy to the despicable acts that went on behind our closed doors. I was his dirty little secret.

My heart breaks every time I think of the most dreadful conversation I overheard my parents having. I was young, but I knew what it meant. It replays vividly in my mind. My father sat my mother down on the living room couch. She was sipping on a glass of her favorite merlot, giving my father her undivided attention.

"Liza, I did some digging into the early years of our relationship."

"Oh really, why?"

"Let me speak! I was so blinded by love, that I didn't' pay attention to detail."

"Detail?"

"Yes, detail! It wasn't until I read the letter that Javon mailed you last month, that I was prompted to do a little research."

"You read my letter? How did you find the letter? It's not what you think!"

"Let's just get right down to it. I had a paternity test done. Do you have anything you'd like to say about that?"

The black walls in the den seemed to somehow get darker. My mother said nothing. The white in her eyes turned red, and a stream of guilt came pouring down her face. My father pleaded.

"Liza, say something."

You could hear a pin drop it was so quiet.

"Speak Liza. Who is TJ's father! We know it's not me bitch. Is it Jovan? According to his letter he seems to think so. He is requesting to meet TJ. TJ is supposed to be

our love child Liza. What have you done to us?"

My mother's body began to shake. Her skin turned a pale beige, and she fell to the floor. My father stood over her for ten minutes repeatedly calling out her name, and kicking her limp body. I just watched. She never got up.

The autopsy confirmed she had been poisoned, and that caused a seizure. However, the report disappeared and there was no proof. Soon after, the pathologist had a stroke, and died at home alone. My mother was cremated before further questions arose.

Thanks to my father's infallible reputation and stature in the business community, he was never suspected of wrong doing. Known for his philanthropy and his love for investing in new innovative start-up companies, my father broke bread with power hitters like politicians and judges. He was a leader with a personal dream team, and I became his secret star player.

Terrified and alone, I knew in that moment what the man I called my father was capable of. I never spoke about what I saw, or what I knew. I just cried myself to sleep night after night. Day by day, I became the monster he taught me to be.

I am a lost soul. After years of therapy and trying every concoction of medicinal regimen you can think of, I realized I was forever broken. He should be the creature I hate most, yet I still feel a longing for his presence.

Hurt people, hurt people, and Lord knows he gifted me with a lifetime of hurt. I paid for the sins of my mother from the moment she left this earth. I can still feel the whistling in the wind as the wet extension cord gets closer to my tailbone. Blow upon blow, I lay in wait for the agonizing pain to overtake my conscious state.

The nightmares will never end. Memories drown my thoughts. The hairs on my arms stand at attention while I reminisce with unmoving intentions. It happened again. I saw everything and did nothing.

Guilty tears fell silently. Sade took my place. In that moment I was not the object of his unforgivable desire. Deafening screams fill the air, radiating through my soul. I let go. Silenced by the freedom of knowing for once, this isn't happening to me. Selfish peace blanketed everything as her soul cried in agony.

I could hear the slight screech of the door opening through the heartbreaking cries for help. The floor began to creek louder, and the sounds of footprints got closer. Peering through the cracks of the closet door, the silhouette of a woman suddenly blocked my view. And, without warning the sound of gunshots echoed through the air. Startled by the piercing ringing, my gasps were masked by Sade's screams. I braced my body against the wall as I slid down and balled up in the fetal position.

I watched as Sade was picked up off the floor and taken into the darkness of the night. No one knew I existed. The master of my torture lay dead on the floor, yet for some reason revenge filled my heart. Through all the unthinkable pain, my tainted heart became obsessed with avenging my father's murder.

Years of counseling and therapy can't erase the hurt of unrequited love given to a child by his father. There were times I felt like nothing more than a secret experiment. An innocent child, poisoned by the chemicals of man while being abused physically, sexually and emotionally. I felt broken beyond repair. The man I saw as my father began killing me slowly the day he found out I wasn't his biological son.

Sade

Caught in the adlibs of the melodies left by my shallow breaths, I knew I wasn't alone. Chills covered my body, and I felt the warmth of prying eyes watching me. Why won't you help me? I feel your presence. Do you see me? The words aren't escaping my body.

I jumped up out of my sleep in a cold sweat. Javier didn't notice thank goodness. Shit. This is the first time I've had this dream in years. My soul has been secretly taunted for many moons. I've always felt like someone was lurking in the shadows, watching my suffering before Victoria burst in guns blazing. No one ever came forward, but the feeling never left me.

Chapter Two

New Beginnings

Sade

I can't wait to see everyone. I haven't planned a celebration for myself in ages. I am long overdue for some much needed adult fun and relaxation. With the twins and my decision to leave the University of Miami, I have so much on my plate. I want to celebrate the good that is happening in my life. I want to climb back out of my shell, shedding my past.

My weekend stay-cations can be rejuvenating, but it's time to celebrate me on another level. My world has changed for the better, and I am tired of hiding my feelings. It's time to embrace my happy, and stop hiding my smile in fear of what other people in this world think. I was not meant to live my life in perpetual mourning.

I love my nanny dearly and would truly be a disaster waiting to happen without her. Grace a is superwoman when it comes to the children. Her milk chocolate skin is flawless. Her smile is brighter than the sun on most days, and her confidence is contagious. At only five feet five inches, she is a tower of inner-strength. Yoga every morning, followed by a power hour of boxing and a minimum of forty-five minutes of writing a day, is what keeps Grace in her personal happy place. She is a disciplined young queen. I admire her passion about her life, not just life, but her life.

I have to admit spending time with Grace helped me grow into a more confident soul, after the Joshua-Antonio fiasco. I began second guessing my decisions like nobody's business, but not so much anymore. Grace helped me shed necessary personal insecurities. It helped me to blossom mentally. I am no longer scared to tell the world how I feel whenever the need arises. Okay well, I wasn't technically scared before, but I'm definitely holding nothing back now.

Pre Grace, I would hold so much in, hiding my true pain for fear my hurt would hurt another. I had to learn that sharing my pain may actually help another to open up and live out loud. Grace is like a little beacon of light, and I am grateful her brilliance shines on me. I don't know everything about her personal life, but she doesn't have my life's diary either.

I met Grace while she was still studying at the University of Miami. She was in school full-time and working as a nanny part-time for the university President.

Grace's resume is stellar. In addition to having years of experience working with youth as a tutor at the private school her parents own, Dartmouth Academy in Manhattan, NY, Grace was a boxing champion. She won a silver medal in the 2016 summer Olympics.

With a Doctorate in Reading and Literacy Education, from the University of Miami, and her physical capabilities, I trust her expertise immensely with the children. It's like having the best of both worlds in one human being. Grace writes poetry and hosts an open mic night on the third Saturday of the month at one of my favorite independent bookstores, Island Books. Island books is located in Key West, Florida. I love to spend hours there on the weekends when I do my stay-cation getaways. It's not too far from home, but far enough that I have to stay and absorb the sea breeze, quiet and serenity. Last time I went, my mini me, Victoria, Cher and Rae joined me. We had a blast. It was a much needed quick getaway.

I started treating myself to stay-cation getaways in the Keys after everything happened with my ex-husband. I found that pouring my all into work and the twins still left me a little anxious. I needed to start doing something that didn't concern work or the children. I just needed to live and enjoy my own company in ways that fuel me passionately.

Grace is off tonight, I invited her to come to my party, and actually party. I want her to let go and enjoy herself. I am so proud of her for all that she's accomplished, and I am grateful for her indescribable loyalty to me and my family. I do wish she would open up a little more about her personal life, but I know what it's like to have skeletons. I don't pry.

Rae will be here at any moment. It's noon and she told me to expect her around lunchtime. She will be the first to arrive, but I have asked all the girls to get ready here with me. I want us to arrive at the party together. They are my strength beyond what I can conceive. When I feel weak it is their spirits that I pull from. Tonight will be no different. I want my sisters in love and life by my side. Tonight will be epic for me.

As *Your Love is Priceless* serenades my silent morning, I smile, swiping my phone in one swift move. It's my angel's ringtone.
"Hello, babe good morning, how are you feeling?" The words floated from my lips effortlessly.
"Good morning sweetheart, how did you sleep?" Javier's voice was deep and alluring.

"Like a baby after you finished ravishing my body."

"Ha! I'm glad I could be of service. Your wish is my command." I knew Javier meant every word.

"My wishes aren't for the faint at heart sir. I'll see you tonight aboard the Bourbon Princess. The question is, are you ready?"

"Ready? What do you mean Sade, I was born ready."

"You know what I mean Javier. Are you ready for us to admit to everyone that we are a couple?"

No words escaped. Just whispered laughter.

"What's so funny mister?"

"What's funny is that you are the one that needs to be ready for tonight's announcements my love, not me. I've been ready to shout to the world how much I am in love with every part of you. You are my queen Sade, and I wake up ready!"

"Oh, okay mister bravery, I got you. Tonight it is then. Smooches my angel, I love you."

"I love you too Sade." And just like that, I am smiling uncontrollably.

Javier has been a blessing in more ways than I can express over this last year. I'm in love, and I'm scared shitless to admit it. Tonight I will shout to the world, mainly my sisters in love and life, how much I love me some him! *I Love Me Some*

Him ... I can hear Toni Braxton singing those words ever so beautifully. I do, love me some Javier.

On my way to the kitchen to get lunch set out for my girls, I heard Rae's motorcycle pull into the driveway. Yes, my girl rides. Rae loves her bike. She usually reserves riding for the weekends. Stephen isn't the happiest about her riding, however he doesn't say much to discourage her. He knows Rae has her own flare. She is all woman, with a little rough neck holstered inside. I pulled the bourbon from behind the bar on my way to the door. I cracked the door open so Rae would know to come on in, and I went back to the kitchen to finish setting lunch out for the ladies. Cher had her assistant bring everything over this morning so I wouldn't have to pick anything up. It is amazing having one of your favorite people in the world be a personal chef. I swear everything she makes is phenomenal.

"Hey!" I heard my Rae singing as she pranced into the kitchen. "How we doing today sis?"
"Better now that you're here Rae."
"Alright now, what do you need me to do first?"
"Girl grab the bourbon glasses out of the cabinet and set them on the counter for me. I want us to eat by the pool, and enjoy the sun before this evening.

Vic and Cher called, they are riding together. They are headed here now."

"No problem Sade, but first I need to run upstairs and lay out my clothes and makeup for today. This way everything is in order since I will be hosting makeover central at your place this evening. I'll be right back to help you get lunch set up." "Love you Rae, thank you." "I am my sister's keeper Sade. I got you."

Rae returned fifteen minutes later, we got everything laid out for the other ladies, and then sat down by the pool to enjoy our first shot of bourbon. As soon as I downed my third shot, Rae blurted out what was really on her mind.

"So when are you going to tell us the lowdown on what's truly happening with you and Javier miss lady?" My mouth dropped to the floor and I was stuck. I got up and walked over to the pool bar to grab the bottle of bourbon. "Girl pick your lip up off the floor. If you think for one second that I don't know that you and Javier are more than friends, you can go somewhere and sit your happy ass back down." Laughing hysterically, Rae continued. "Woman, I am ready, set and go all in one when it comes to you, Vic and Cher. Stop acting surprised. I know what I know Sade. Now the real question is, when do you plan to tell all of us what I already know?"

There's no dodging Rae when she's like this. "And that's why I love you Rae. Straight no chaser all day every day." I looked her square in her eyes, and I took two more shots before continuing to respond. "Yes, I got you Rae." "You got me, then stop all that nervous laughter, and start spilling the tea Sade."

My phone chimed. It was a message from Vic letting me know she and Cher were close. The message interrupted my thoughts, and I changed the subject letting Rae know the girls were close. I began to wonder, if Rae knew, did they all already know? Was everyone aware? No way. Javier and I had been very discrete to ensure we had plenty of alone time and energy to get to know each other intimately. It has been a pleasure learning the good, bad and ugly about Javier. We truly took the time to break down each other's surface glow and hone in on what lies beneath. I can honestly say that I love every intricate detail of Javier's being. We deserve to be happy and I am finally ready to live out loud again.

Rae grabbed my phone from the table as soon as my favorite song started signing. "Hmmm, *Your Love is Priceless* huh, I wonder who that is?" Rae took off and started running around the pool just as I went to grab for it.

"Sis, come on, answer it if you're not going to give it to me." Rae read the love and want on my face and tossed me the phone. "Nope sis, I won't steel your thunder. I will wait until you decide to tell the masses. Just know Sade, I know what I know." "I love you too Rae."

How could my love not run soul deep for Rae? No matter how secretive and shy we tried to be, Rae always knew what was really up with each of us. She's that friend, she just knows. And believe me, she *ain't* never scared.

I heard my sister's car turn into the drive blasting her music. Rae and I both hurried to the door with two glasses of bourbon in hand each. Vic unlocked the door with her key.

"It's about time!" Rae screamed.
Rae and I handed the ladies a shot of bourbon and helped them inside. "I'll have a triple of what you're having. I need to be just as chill and relaxed as you and Rae are right now." Cher was ready to let loose. "Yes, I'm with Cher!" Vic agreed.
Rae and I replied at the same time. "I'm on it. Get your asses in a swim suit and meet us by the pool." I hurried them along and refilled all the glasses.

Chapter Three
Spill It

Sade

"Damn sis! Vic, you look amazing in your new swim suit. I can't wait to order from your upcoming summer collection." "Why thank you Sade." "You're more than welcome hot mama. It's cool though. Rae will have this body in tip top shape by summer. She's been my personal trainer for the last six months. Rae's so good in the gym. You know she trains others as a side hustle. I figured why not me too. I just have a little more work to do before I reach my workout goals." "Thank you again Sade, but you know damn well you could fiercely rock this swimsuit right now with those killer curves!" "Ha, I love you Vic." "Yes ma'am, I love you too big sis."

Oh great, Vic has one of those I know something you don't know looks again. "What are you up to Vic. I see it in your eyes." "You all should already know how I move. Of course I have a one-of-a-kind swimsuit set aside, designed in your favorite colors. You will all rock the runway as my finale models at the close of my first semi-annual fashion show. Artistry will host a winter show in December and a summer show in July."

"I'm so proud of you Vic, we all are."

Cher lifted her glass high, and continued. "Here's to new beginnings, perseverance, independence, entrepreneurship and true love." As Cher said *true love*, all of our glasses met in the middle, and all eyes were on me.

Wow. Okay how do I start this conversation. I mean do I just blurt it out, or do I ease into it. I know everyone thought I was so fragile for a while. I hope they know I have thoroughly thought this through. I know what I want, and I want Javier. I should just say that. I should say something. Anything. Silence blanketed the air. All eyes still on me for what seemed like eternity. I snapped out of my personal intersession thanks to Rae's nudge.

"I have something personal I want to share with everyone, and I don't know where to begin. I will just start with the end. I am in love." Silence again, and then Victoria began to prance around me looking me up and down. "In love, did you say you're in love?" "Yes, little sis, I am in love."

Vic looked at Cher and Rae and then back at me. She had the most serious look on her face. She walked to the pool bar, poured a double and took a deep breath. I watched, waiting for her to say something else. There was an awkward silence for a minute and then she locked eyes with Cher and

Rae as they turned to me. With their free hand they all reached for me. Vic continued.

"My sweet Sade, I am your little sister. I am my sister's keeper. You had to know that I knew you and Javier were dating. I am always watching. Sis, we all are. You know our resident chemist, inspector Rae, and secret agent Cher have been on the case since your first date." "Our first date." I replied in shock. "Yes big sis, since your first date. We haven't mentioned anything to our men, but I'm sure if they are as in tune to Javier as we are to you, they know."

"Okay Vic, if you all know where we went on our first date, do tell." My girls smiled and motioned for me to sit. It seems there was no secret to be had. They never skip a beat.

Cher explained. "Javier ordered a catered dinner from House of Cher. He probably thought I was off because I was supposed to be, but one of my managers called out that day, and I decided to work. Javier called and placed the order under one of his private investigator aliases, but didn't realize I was working that day. I answered the phone and actually took the order. Of course I recognized Javier's voice immediately, but didn't ruin his anonymity. When he ordered your all-time favorite, my famous baked lasagna with fresh garlic bread and a small antipasto salad with extra red wine Italian vinaigrette for two, I knew who his date was. I took extra care to make sure the order was perfect without saying a word to you or Javier. I included desert for two as a gift for being a repeat customer. The order was delivered to the Presidential Penthouse at the Aria Hotel and Spa on Fisher Island."

Coming up for air, Cher grabbed my hands and looked at me with sincerity and love in her eyes. With Vic and Rae at my side, Cher kept going. "I told Victoria and Rae because I was happy for you two. I vowed them to secrecy, and we promised to keep an eye on you. Sade, we just wanted you to live and be happy exploring the possibilities of love again."

Vic took over where Cher left off. "I was scared for you myself, Sade, but Cher and Rae reminded me that my big sister is a fierce, brilliant woman who deserves to be happy in love again. So I paid attention, we all did, in silence. We knew eventually you'd open up to us. Now, I didn't think it would take this long, but I knew you would tell us everything when you were ready."

What a relief. The only people's opinion I would consider about my personal life already know. They've known about my precious Javier since the beginning. It feels like a ton of weights have been lifted from my shoulders.

"Say something Sade," Vic nudged. "I love you all so very much for loving me the way you do. My sisters in life, you are a blessing to my soul. These are tears of joy you see streaming down my face. I hoped you'd all be happy for me. I was afraid you wouldn't think I was ready, or that Javier was a rebound." "That's just it Sade." "What is it Rae?" "Whatever this is or isn't for you Sade, I am always here. I am my sister's keep, we all are!" Rae's words landed with conviction.

"Cheers to new beginnings ladies. Javier makes me happy, he comforts me in the depth of the night when my fears resurface. He listens and supports my dreams. Instead of complaining about problems, he's the one there ready to offer solutions." I saw Cher giving me the side eye, and I knew what was next.

"So missy, what else has Javier done to keep that smile on your face?" "I see you Cher, and to answer your question, everything. With every stroke I lose control. He hits every spot I never knew I had." "Alright now, every spot you never knew you had. That's what I'm talking about Sade."

"Yes, Cher it fills me up every morning. It's like we've known each other our entire life. He knows how to ignite my naughty in the best way." "Stella has definitely got her groove back." "Shut up Rae, you're hilarious. Alright ladies it's my night to enjoy the man who had the patience and faith to believe in me when I was too weak to do it for myself."

"We are here to celebrate you sis, and I am glad you're finally in a place where you are comfortable living out loud again." "Thank you Vic. Now, let's hit the hot tub for a bit and enjoy our lunch." Arm in arm we sauntered over to the hot tub.

My sister-friends are the absolute best. What did I do to deserve these women. I'm so grateful for their presence.

We were reminiscing about some of our wild times together while relaxing in the hot tub when the doorbell rang. It snapped us out of our girls trip down memory lane. Cher popped up. "I'll get it honey, just relax." "Thanks Cher." Cher walked back out with a bouquet of flowers so big we could not see half of her body.

"Wow! There's a card." Rae's voice was on ten. She admired the bouquet, snatched the card and gave it to me.

Dear Sade,

I love you with all my soul, and I can't wait to let the world know. I hope you're still ready. If you aren't we will wait until you are, but I pray you're ready. I have waited for years to find my queen, and I feel like life has given us a second chance. You deserve to be loved unconditionally, and I am honored to be the man at your side making sure all of your needs are met. We will continue to build together, and know that you will never have to wonder about my love. Action is everything, and I will continue to wake each day determined to keep a smile on your face. I love you angel. I can't wait to see your stunning face this evening.

Javier

"Sade, his words are beautiful." "Oh but even better sis, his actions prove all that he says. Vic, I've never felt so loved, so seen. He studies me and finds joy in seeing me succeed. Javier is so attentive, and I appreciate every bit of it."

"We are all happy for you Sade. We are so ready to celebrate with you both. All the goodness you've experienced in this last year is well deserved. You are a warrior. I will always look up to you. I have since I was born. I love you Sade." "I love you more Vic."

"Okay enough with the mushiness." Rae smized at us like Tyra Banks with her big beautiful eyes and continued. "Let's get these speakers blasting again so we can finish our day party. I will be ready to start makeup on you queens at 6:30 this evening. So that gives us a few more hours of fun in the sun. We must all be glammed up and ready to rip the runway by 8:30 tonight."

I can't wait either. Well I can a little. I am having the time of my life. My girls are the best. Feeling a little fiery energy boiling in my soul, I put on some old school Miami base, and we got it in. Popping it every way from Sunday, as my grandmother used to say. The music was so loud we must not have heard the doorbell ring. When I looked up at the camera, I noticed someone walking away from the door. I ran to the door, but by the time I got there, the person was gone. There was a large rectangular box leaning against the door. When I closed the door and got to the hallway, all the ladies were standing there waiting for me.

"What? Why is everyone staring at me." "We are curious, what's in the box Sade?" "I have no idea Cher." "Open it!" Vic and Rae shouted at the same time. "There is no return address on the box. What do you think it is. This is weird girls." "Just open the box already Sade." "Okay Cher, I am. I just wish I knew who the hell it was from, and why there's no return address." "If you don't open this box so we can figure out the mystery together, I am going to rip it open for you." Rae reached for the box. "Rae stop, I got it."

Vic started to tear up as I opened the box. I caught a glimpse of her out of the corner of my eye. So intrigued, I ripped the box open and we all gasped at the same time. Well everyone but Vic that is. She stood there staring at me with tears streaming down her face. I let the box go and Rae held on to it for me. I turned to Vic and picked her up in my arms. Spinning her around screaming thank you is so not enough, but that's what I did for the next ten minutes.

"It's beautiful Victoria when did you have the time to do this? How did you keep this from me? Who delivered it? This gown is stunning sis. Oh my God, I am in awe. You're a genius designer. I cannot wait to try it on. Javier is going to love me in this tonight. I feel like such a queen. Thank you. Thank you. Thank you."

"Sade you are so very welcome. I pray it fits like a glove. You should know that Javier hired me three months ago to design this dress exclusively for you. It took everything for me not to share this with you. He wanted it to be a surprise. Seeing the look on your face and the joy in your eyes, I know this was a secret worth keeping. Javier is such a thoughtful soul sis. He loves you so unapologetically."

"This is an amazing surprise Vic. You truly are your sister's keeper. Baby sis, I don't ever want to imagine a world with you not at my side. Thank you a million times over." "You're welcome Sade."

This made my day, I feel like a teenager laying eyes on her prom dress for the first time. "Wow. You little ladies had me around here thinking I had secrets in the bag, and you knew all along. I appreciate you all for being willing to wait until I was ready to share."

Cher's eyes welled with tears as she spoke. "Sade, we love you and only want what's best for you. When you were dealing with the Joshua-Antonio situation, I saw the way Javier's eyes were watching you. There's no mountain he wouldn't have moved to protect you, or give you what you needed. We all noticed it. I am grateful that you have one another."

Rae nodded in agreeance with Cher, kissed me on my forehead and turned the music back up. We danced our hearts out for another hour and enjoyed a few more shots of bourbon.

Chapter Four

She Chose Me

Javier

I have waited for this day since the first time I met Sade many moons ago. On one hand, I felt blessed to be enjoying coffee and our conversation. On the other hand, I felt deflated because she turned down my request for a second date. Now years later, she is the love of my life.
After everything ended with the Antonio saga, Sade was extremely withdrawn. She trusted no one, and I can't blame her. I worked tirelessly to make sure everyone's name was cleared from any wrong doing on our part. Every decision made was in self-defense and for the preservation of our lives.

During the initial weeks following the incident, I spent the night in Sade's guest house to offer protection. I convinced her that living on the property alone so soon after the killings was not safe for her. Sade didn't want to live with Victoria and Pierre as planned. She wanted to be in the privacy of her own home to mourn in peace. I understood that, so I offered the compromise to Vic and Pierre to ease their hearts.

Their mother Ms. Sophia spends half her time at Vic's house, and the other half of her time at Sade's house. She has everything she needs at both homes so she moves back and forth with ease. Ms. Sophia and Vic took on the majority of the parenting responsibilities for the twins for the first couple of months to give Sade time to breathe. Sade's spirit brightened after she decided not to return to the university. She made a decision pursue her entrepreneurial goals. Our conversations got longer and longer with each new encounter. On Sundays I would go to my place, make sure everything was clean and do my laundry. After weeks of staying in Sade's guest house, she surprised me. I returned to Sade's from my place one Sunday, and Sade called out for me from the main house. She asked me to come over. I dropped my clean laundry off inside the guest house and did as she requested. As I approached, the aroma coming from the kitchen window had my mouth watering. Sade had whipped up a feast fit for a king, and invited me to join her. I can still here her as if it were yesterday.

> *"Javier, you have been a blessing to me. Your presence, however quiet, brings me comfort. Knowing that you are here has helped me sleep an extra few minutes each night. Last night, for the first time since I can remember, I slept from midnight till sunrise. For me that was a miracle."*

I responded to her leaving my heart on my sleeve.

"Sade, I am here for you as long as you need me. I meant what I said the day I moved into the guest house. I could not live with myself if anything happened to you knowing what you've endured."

There was always a sweetness to Sade's tone when speaking to me.

"Javier, I appreciate you being here. I Sometimes I look up, see your smiling face, gentle eyes and breathe a little easier. Between my gradual peace of mind at home, and my workouts with Rae, the numbness is beginning to fade."

I stayed for dinner that evening. We had garlic and herb seasoned grilled tuna steak, roasted red potatoes with peppers, asparagus, mashed potatoes with goat cheese, and homemade peach whiskey pound cake for dessert. Sade could throw down in the kitchen and she always used the veggies from her garden. I love watching her pick vegetables from the garden. Everything was delicious.

That evening was a new beginning for both of us. We talked for hours that night and every night thereafter. Sunday dinners turned into Monday movie nights, whiskey Wednesday nights by the pool, Friday night dancing at my brother's club and Saturdays at the beach with pizza and bourbon. It's hard to say when the lines blurred for our feelings, but everything happened naturally. I let Sade set the pace for our relationship. Slowly but surely I watched in awe as her strength helped her to persevere. Sade let me into the darkest corners of her mind unleashing the beast that has caused her nightmares for years. She described every intricate detail of the final night she was brutally raped by Theodore. She even trusted me with the truth behind her survival. I know it happened more than once, but I never pushed for more information than she was willing to share freely.

Sharing the most intimate parts of her past, only made me fall deeper for Sade. I fell in love, and for the first time in my life, I didn't want to run from it. I had avoided love like the plague for years. But with Sade, I wasn't in control. My heart was hers before my mind had a chance to decide. We didn't share our relationship status with anyone. We stayed off the beaten path to avoid running into our friends and family. Neither of us wanted to talk about our relationship with anyone. We just wanted to live in our own bubble for a while. Our first formal date was on a Tuesday evening. I ordered take out from House of Cher. I made sure

Cher was off that evening. I called in and ordered all of Sade's favorites to go. I rented a beach house for two days on Fisher Island. We had a quiet candlelit dinner by the pool on our first night. Then we enjoyed a couples massage under the stars. We spent the next two days soaking up the sun, hanging out on the boardwalk, listening to live music and being lost in each other's everything.

We haven't looked back since. Now we are ready to share our story with family and friends. I hope everyone is accepting. I know they love us both individually, I just pray they are okay with us together. I intend to spend the rest of my life with Sade. It would be nice to have the blessing of our loved ones.

Hanging out with the boys has gotten harder since I can never talk about who I'm dating. Usually I would be able to chime in, and add a little single and dating spice to the conversation. That hasn't happened in a while. When they start probing me for what's happening in my love life, I tell them that I haven't had time to worry about it. I blame everything on my work load. I had to become the king of changing the conversation. I'm not sure if it worked, but no one ever questioned me.

I'm just ready to get everything out in the open so Sade and I can love out loud. I'm tired of being silent when my boys boast about their amazing wives and significant others. I respect Sade, and I understood her need for privacy. Letting her take the lead where we are concerned was best for both of us. I didn't have to worry about overstepping, and she only took on as much as she could handle.

I wonder if the rest of our crew really has a clue about how strong my woman is. Sade has endured so much pain in her life. The night she broke down and shared with me about Theodore I wanted to kill every being in sight. I didn't even know who she was at that time in her life, but I wish I could have been there to save her from that trifling bastard. If he wasn't killed then, he would have been dead within minutes after I found out what he did to Sade! The images in my mind of me slicing and dicing Theodore to shreds were interrupted by the continuous chiming of my doorbell.

"Okay I'm coming! Who is it?" "Open the damn door a familiar voice echoed from the other side."

It sounds like Matthew, but the guys aren't supposed to be stopping by until later. We are all heading to the party together to celebrate tonight.

The ladies are doing their thing together, so the fellas always include me in their roundup.

When I opened the door, Matthew, Stephen and Pierre were staring me in the face. They quickly pushed me aside and rushed in.

"What the Fuck? What's up with you guys. Why are you all looking at me like death just pulled your card?"

No one said anything, but I knew something was wrong because of the look in Mathew's eyes.

"Sit down Javier." Pierre's tone was deliberate. "Okay I'm sitting Pierre. What is going on?" Pierre looked at me and then pointed at Stephen.

On que, Stephen began to explain. "The issue is Theodore's son. He has managed to reopen the case of his father's murder after new evidence has been found." "What the hell are you talking about Stephen?"

"Javier, I'll explain. I got this Stephen, he deserves to hear this from me." The intensity in my eyes was fueled by anger not shock, and before he started speaking, Pierre figured that out. His return glare let me know that he knew there was no secret to tell.

"Pierre, I know about the rape. I know about Theodore and the circumstances surrounding his death. Sade confided in me, and swore me to secrecy. I assume Victoria did the same to you."

Shocked, Pierre nodded and began to explain. "Javier, I had to break my silence and tell our boys. Victoria started getting harassing phone calls and didn't want anyone to know at first. After about a month of non-stop calls, she finally broke down and told me what was going on."

"What the hell is going on Pierre?" "Let me finish Javier. Theodore apparently had a son. His son has been calling Victoria, leaving her threatening messages. He claims to know what really happened to his father. He has threatened to rape my wife, and kill her the way she killed his father."

"That motherfucker! Wasn't Sade's father friends with Theodore? Or at least wouldn't he have known whether or not Theodore had children? According to Victoria he didn't have children."

My heart was beating so fast I began to gasp for air. I was infuriated. "Calm down Javier, right now we need your expertise and connections to find this bastard. He has decided to rear his ugly head after all these years." My muscles started tightening as I envisioned squeezing the life out of Theodore's son.

"Pierre, I will murder that prick, and bury his body before any of you notice he's gone. What's his name? What's his damn name!" Knowing I meant every word, the fellas were right on my heels as I headed straight for my office. I turned on the computer, and demanded to know everything they could tell me about the messages Vic was receiving. Calm is the last thing I can be.

"His name is Ratcliff Theodore Jameson." Pierre glared at me and continued. "From what I've been able to gather, he goes by TJ."

"He should be going by Rat!" "I agree Javier, but we have to focus. We need you to find his ass so we can bury him, and protect the women we love."

Stephen began to pace back and forth. I tried to type as fast as possible. My fingers were giving the keys a brutal beating. His eyes began to squint which meant his wheels were ready for takeoff. Then the mumbling started. "I'll fly us around the world. We will find that snake Javier and Pierre, don't worry. We'll get him."

"Yes, you're damn right Stephen, we will get him.'' Mathew's voice echoed off the walls."

"Bingo! One of my contacts just messaged me. The last call pinged from a cell tower within three miles of Cher's home on the island."

Pierre glared at me. "Damn Javier that was fast."
"Yeah Pierre, I wish Vic had come forth immediately, but I'll find his ass, never doubt that my brother."

Puzzled, we all just looked at one another in shock. "Wait!" Mathew spoke with intent. "He must have gained access to our celebration itinerary for the weekend. Perhaps he knows we are planning to be on the island for brunch tomorrow at Cher's. Oh shit, Cher has been back and forth to the island alone so much over the past two weeks. What if he's been watching my woman? I'll slaughter him."

Standing up from the computer I felt numb again. Matthew and Stephen stepped up behind me. "We got you Javier. Believe it or not, we already know." "Know what Matthew?"

Mathew cleared his throat and squared off with me. Eye to eye, he spoke to me unapologetically. "Javier, we all know about you and Sade. We've just chosen not to pry because we trust you man. We know she's in good hands with you. We knew eventually you'd both be confident enough to share your story with us openly. All of us knew tonight was your coming out party, and we were so excited to finally congratulate you and Sade. We still will. Theodore nor his off spring will ruin tonight for Sade. She deserves this. You deserve this too Javier."

"Thank you my brother. Matthew, I appreciate you. I appreciate all of you. Shit's just crazy."

Chapter Five

Nightmares and Terrors

Victoria

My heart melted seeing the look on Sade's face when she saw the gown I designed for her party. I've tried so hard to focus solely on her today. Her happiness is all that matters right now. It would kill her to know what I have been suffering through. I don't want her to know. I need another shot of bourbon and some snap out of it music to calm my roaring thoughts.

Sade and I have been through so much in our lifetime. After surviving the Joshua-Antonio disaster, I naively thought maybe, just maybe, we could move on and never look back. The past, however always has a knack for finding its way to my present and terrorizing my soul. I've been getting these outlandish calls from Theodore's son. My family always thought that Theodore didn't have children. He never brought a child around my father's office or our home. Apparently we were wrong. Theodore's so called son has been leaving me cryptic messages claiming to know what I did to his father. He also threatened to rape me while forcing my sister to watch. Then he told me he'd kill us both in cold blood the way his father was gunned down.

I was in shock, I was fifteen at the time. It was a lifetime ago. Why now? After a while I couldn't take it anymore. I had to let Pierre know what was going on. I knew I couldn't handle this on my own. I began to have nightmares so routinely I dread falling asleep. I haven't shared any of this with Sade or the girls. Pierre is only privy to the information because I couldn't lie to him. He knew I wasn't fine although I said that I was. He read my actions, which did not match my words. Almost every night for at least a month, he's had to sit up with me after I wake from a screaming nightmare. There's only so much he can take. I finally broke down and told him all the gory details. Everyone found out about the rape when Sade blurted it out during the ordeal with her ex-husband, but not everyone knew what happened to Theodore. We swore each other to secrecy till death.

Now Pierre knows all the gory details of our secret, more importantly what I did. It's been extremely difficult to focus on work. My designs and Artistry have taken a back seat in the past month. I am exhausted from lack of sleep due to the stress that is consuming me. I try so hard to keep it together when I am around the family or our girls. Sometimes I fall short and just blame it on work. Excuses don't work well with my girls.

We know each other too well. Sade already told me that Rae called her, and shared her concerns about me taking on too much professionally. Rae knows my moods like the back of her hand, and she'll keep digging if necessary to find out what has me off kilter.

Even Cher knows something's not right with me. She made dinner for us a couple of weeks ago, and stopped by to drop it off. She said she was trying out a new dish and wanted our opinion. I knew she read the stress on my face. Cooking is always her way to calm the nerves and lend a hand. That night was slightly more peaceful thanks to her efforts. My mind didn't race as much, at least not until I drifted off to sleep.

"Victoria! Snap out of it. It's time to get ready for the party. Remember, Rae said she wanted to start makeup at 6:30 this evening."
Sade's voice jolted me back to present. I can't let Theodore or his offspring ruin tonight for Sade and Javier. I have to get my thoughts together. My mind keeps drifting back to the awful night that I murdered Theodore.

"I got you Sade. I'm headed back outside to the pool bar to grab some of the sushi Cher made, and then I'll be right up."
Sade winked, and gestured for me to hurry.

Rae peeped outside and saw me sitting at the bar. I was in mid chew when she sat down next to me.

"Are you okay Vic?" "Yes Rae, I'm fine. I just want this evening to go smoothly for Sade."

"I know there is more going on in that head of yours than assuring that Sade has a great party. I can tell by the vacant look in your eyes that you are a million miles away. Sooner or later I will get to the bottom of it. You know I will."

"I'm fine Rae! I don't need you to psychoanalyze me. Let's head up and get our showers so you can work wonders on our faces." "No problem Vic. All is tabled for now, but I will find out what's eating away at you."

Rae is correct. I can't keep this all bottled up inside, but today is not the day. I can't wait to see my big sister walk out in her striking gown. A breathtaking beauty, my sweet Sade surely could have been a runway model.

Sade had the music serenading us throughout the house while we enjoyed our hot showers and started getting ready for the party.
I made myself a new elegant pant jumpsuit for Sade's party. It's royal blue and fits me like a glove. It gives off Jaquelyn Kennedy first lady vibes.

I will be rocking my hot pink stilettos from the Sassy collection. I bought a pair for Sade's dress also. I'll give them to her when she gets out of the shower. Sassy Boutique is my new online go to when I want a pair of fierce heels. I will be partnering with them when I host my next fashion show.

By the time we all finished our showers, Rae was ready to start. Cher is first. She won't be riding with us to the party. Unfortunately, her assistant called in sick this morning. Cher decided to head over a little early to ensure everything is set up as expected. Cher is going to be wearing the black catsuit with the stunning low cut neckline embossed in black pearls that I made for her. It was a gift made in love. It was my way of saying thank you for being so supportive of my entrepreneurial endeavors. She has been a great friend and mentor. I love her dearly.

I can't wait to see Rae in the gown that I made her. The strapless sweetheart top is elegant. The gown hugs her curves in all the right places, accentuating her coke bottle physique.
For the first time since I've started my own fashion house, all of my girls will be wearing something I have exclusively designed for them. I am honored and excited. I just hope I can keep my thoughts in

check. This is Sade's moment, not Theodore's. Thank goodness I have Pierre to lean on. I hate that I had to tell him more in depth details about what happened, but his support is invaluable. He is my rock.

"Alright Vic you're up next. Park it." "Yes ma'am Rae, you're a miracle worker."

I sat there, took a couple deep breaths and let Rae transform me. We all paused as Cher waltzed back into the guest room where Rae's beauty bar was set up. She looked stunning.

"Yes, Cher you look fabulous darling!" Sade circled Cher repeating herself a few more times. We all were in awe of Cher's elegance. Tonight was sure to be an evening to remember. My sister deserves to celebrate her love and feel like she can live out loud.

"Okay my lovelies, I am headed over to my place to check on the set up and food for the evening. The DJ has already arrived and he's grooving nicely. I have someone outside to valet the cars for our guests so they may be dropped off at the door. The vacant lot next to my estate is being used for tonight's parking."

"Cher, I truly appreciate you doing all of this for me tonight. It means the world to me." "It's my pleasure Sade, my pleasure."

Cher's phone started serenading us. We knew it was Matthew by the song, All I do is Think of You by Troop. It's one of Cher's all-time favorite songs, so of course it's Matthew's ringtone. She has the tendency to switch his ringtones to different love songs that she adores. She answered right away. Those two are so adorable together.

"That was Matthew." In unison we all replied, "We know Cher." "Ha, you all got jokes. Okay. Well, Matthew called to let me know that he and the fellas will be heading over within the next thirty minutes. I will see you ladies shortly. It's one hour till showtime." Cher smiled, told us to get a move on it and air kissed us goodbye.

Chapter Six

Love Out Loud

Sade

Between Victoria's designs and Rae's makeover, we all looked like royalty. I can't wait to lay eyes on Javier. I hope he thinks I am as beautiful as I feel in this moment.

"You're our blessing Rae. We all look like queens ready to take the throne."

"Yes we do Sade. You can't tell me anything. I feel like a supermodel rocking one of Victoria's couture designs." Rae meant every word. She spun around in the mirror a few times and struck a pose.

"I'm so happy you love them." Victoria's teared up as spoke. Seeing her designs in motion must be such an exhilarating feeling. "Got me over here tearing up and blushing like a school girl. You ladies look fabulous! I had so much fun designing them for you. I am most at peace, as you all know, when I am designing. It helps too, that my girls are such gorgeous muses."

I have to make sure I don't leave my surprises for the girls. I bought the ladies a special treat for always being at my side. I placed it in my white silk shoulder bag with the rest of my surprises for the evening. I can't wait to show Javier what I have in store for him later tonight.

"Sade, ladies, the limo driver just arrived. Let's have one last toast. We are going to switch it up a bit. Grab a glass of champagne instead of bourbon. I placed a glass for everyone right there on the counter. Cheers to my big sister for feeling confident enough to celebrate her life and to love out loud."

"Thank you Vic, you're the best little sister a girl could have. You all have been amazing to me. Your love and support is everything."
We all air kissed and sauntered to the limo.

"Finally, we're here, and a little early too. Let the partying begin ladies." There was definitely extra pep in my step thanks to Javier. "Lead the way Sade, you are the queen for the evening."
"Oh, I'm the queen every day Princess Victoria."

Grace just arrived. I am so glad she came. She's such an integral part of my healing process. Her support with the children and her friendship is invaluable. She's been a bit distant lately, but her support with the twins hasn't wavered.

"Hey gorgeous ladies!" Grace smiled and leaned in to give each of us a hug. Her usually calming energy was coming off a little tense.

"Grace, you look fabulous doll. I am so glad you made it. I've got a little something in store for you this evening." Perhaps my surprise will ease whatever is occupying Grace's mind. "Sade, of course I would be here. There's no place I'd rather be. You deserve to celebrate, and you know how much I care about you and the children."

Cher opened the door and motioned for us to get inside. "We made it. Where are the fellas?" "They're outside mingling and enjoying the cocktail hour. We started serving and entertaining a few minutes early since a couple of guests have already arrived." "Thank you Cher." "Always Sade, we got you. I have to run into the kitchen and speak with the chef. I'll see you ladies in a few. Smooches." Cher is a Godsent gift to our soul.

"You all look stunning ladies." "Thank you Matthew, we love you too." "You're welcome. Shall I escort you ladies outside? The fellas and I were out here entertaining the early guests."

As soon as the we stepped onto the back patio, the vibe was inviting. Cher had thought of everything. There was a smorgasbord of delicious cuisine being served. The champagne fountain was flowing, and the chocolate fountain was screaming my name. I walked over to the DJ and let him know what time I wanted to speak to the guests. He nodded and went back to spinning good vibes.

It's nothing like old school Disc Jockey's that still spin vinyl.

I danced my way over to my man and hugged him from behind. He spun around and held my hands out toward him. "You look absolutely stunning my queen." "Thank you Javier, you look quite handsome yourself my love."

"Mom is upstairs settling the twins in dear, and I have to tell Vic that Daniel came. He was the first to arrive after we pulled up." "That's wonderful Javier. Oh, I see him now. And Vic just spotted him too. Daniel looks nice. I am so glad he was able to come. I hope he is able to enjoy himself. He deserves it. Daniel has been a trusted board member at Artistry since it opened. He has been a loyal friend and colleague to Victoria."

"I am glad he came too Sade. He's a good man. Taking care of his mother isn't easy, but he never complains. Let's mingle. We will start with Daniel and work our way around."

Javier grabbed two glasses of champagne for us, and we worked the party. It was so nice to see everyone. Guests were steadily arriving and everyone seemed to be having a great time. It feels so good to celebrate being happy again and feeling loved unconditionally. We partied our tails off for a couple of hours and then I invaded the DJ booth.

"Mic check one two, one two. Can you beautiful souls hear me? Hello and thank you for coming. The night is still young, but I wanted to take this opportunity to thank you for being here. If you've been invited to celebrate with me this evening, it's because you have been a positive force in my life. I thank you from the depths of my soul. Please know that you are all appreciated."

I hear you're welcome echoing through the crowd. It is surreal to be celebrating. My heart is overcome with joy.

"To my baby sister Victoria, and my sisters in life, Rae and Cher, words or things could never truly express how blessed I feel to have you in my life." "We love you too." Rae shouted.

"Come up closer for a moment ladies, I have a special gift for you." I handed them each a small yellow silk drawstring bag. They tore into them immediately. The look on their faces when they pulled out matching diamond tennis bracelets was priceless.

"If you turn them over ladies, you'll see that your name, and I am my sister's keeper is engraved underneath." They rushed towards me and gathered me into a group hug, showering me with kisses. I wiggled free and continued.

"Okay, for the next surprise, mommy and Victoria this is for you." Victoria passed the envelop to our mother to open it. She was so excited to find a weekend spa package for the two of them. "Now don't think you're going without me, I will be right there with you. We will work together to plan the perfect weekend." Mommy hugged me so tight. I could feel her love radiating through my body.

"Grace, can you come forward please. I have a little something for you too. Thank you for being a phenomenal nanny, teacher and mentor to the children. I too thank you for being a friend. This is for you." Grace kissed me on the cheek and thanked me. She opened it, and the tears began to stream down her face. We had been scouting areas to open up a beachside seafood bar. We found one that we fell in love with about two months ago. We visited the property a couple of times. When I was sure Grace loved it, I set up a private meeting with a commercial realtor. As of last Friday, I am the new owner of the property. I bought it outright.

"Oh my goodness Sade! You bought our bar." Grace's arms flew around my neck, and she cried out with excitement. "Yes, I did madam general manager. The keys in your hand are yours. I've got my set already. We can discuss everything further in a few days." Applause filled the night air.

"Now, before we get back to partying, I'd like to share this space with the new love of my life." Javier stepped up beside me. Placed his arm around my waist and laid the softest kiss on my forehead. "Please raise your glasses as I toast this handsome man that I love with my entire being. Javier, you have knelt with me, praying in the trenches. You have been a warrior, always having my back. I am honored to stand at your side and continue this journey of love with you. Thank you for being the reason I am able to love out loud again. Cheers to you my king."

Javier wrapped me in his arms and slid the microphone from my hands. "Sade, you are the love of my life. Thank you for letting me in. You are my everything. I love you, and I look forward to a lifetime of memories with you."

"Cheers to Javier and Sade," Victoria sang at the top of her lungs. We all clinked our glasses. Javier signaled for the DJ to turn the music back up. We got down and walked to the pool bar to spend time with the gang. Cher, Rae, Vic, Matthew and Pierre were waiting with grins plastered on their faces larger than the state of Texas.

"Welcome to the family my brother." "Thanks Pierre, I appreciate you man." "Javier, I couldn't have hoped for a better partner for my sister. Maybe someday you will be my brother-in-law." Oh no, I could see the dreamy look in my sister's eyes. Victoria was seeing wedding bells.

"Thank you Victoria. I love you like a little sister already. Our future awaits. One thing is for certain, I'm not going anywhere. I love Sade with all my soul."

Stephen popped off his bar stool, took Rae by the hand and led the way. "Let's go everyone it's time for the soul train line. We have more partying to do!" Rae started us off with her famous Rerun dance moves and we had the time of our lives. We danced until our feet couldn't take anymore. It felt great to just let go.

Vic and Pierre headed to the chocolate fountain about thirty minutes ago, and I haven't seen them since. I wonder where they are. Vic seemed a little distant tonight. She put on an Oscar winning front, but I know my little sister. Something is eating away at her and I will figure out what it is.

"Sade, what are you thinking about darling?" "Just how grateful I am Rae. I appreciate having you all in my life. Has anyone noticed that Victoria seems a little off? Something is going on with my little sister. I can't stop thinking about it?" "Yes Sade, we have noticed. Cher and I just didn't want to bring it up today. You know Vic would never let us focus on her when we are supposed to be celebrating you." Javier put his arm around my shoulder and pulled me closer to him.

"Victoria will be okay my love. We will check on her in forty-eight hours. We can stop by the house after our return and talk to her. As for now, you are all mine." "Yes Javier, I'm all yours." Javier is right I should only be focused on the two of us for now.

"We got Vic, you don't have to worry about her. You two love birds have some alone time in the Bahamas waiting for you." "Thanks for being reassuring Stephen."

Javier and Stephen embraced in a brotherly hug. Matthew and the girls nodded in agreeance with Stephen. Javier stood up, and helped me from my chair. We hugged everyone goodbye, thanked them for a night to remember and headed to the Bourbon Princess.

"We will call you if anything comes up. For now just focus on yourselves and nothing else."

We changed and sat on the deck to unwind. Javier passed me a glass of champagne and we star gazed together. The stars were illuminating the night sky. It was breathtakingly beautiful and peaceful. Within twenty minutes, we set sail for a paradise. We should arrive shortly after breakfast. Above all else Javier and I were happy to no longer have to keep our love for each other a secret. It seems it was an act in futility when it comes to our crew anyway. My girls had figured it out on their own, and the guys didn't seem too surprised either.

"Javier, did the guys already know we were together? Cher, Vic and Rae let me know today that they have known for months." Javier smiled. Gently placing his hand under my chin, he pulled me in for a kiss. "Yes Sade, they knew."

Chapter Seven

Paradise

Sade

Still eyes are watching over me as I sleep. Unlike in the past, this time it feels like a blessing. The protective armor of Javier's love covers me. The rising sun warms my face, and the subtle breeze from the coast awakens my senses. Peacefulness consumes the air. I am happy. I feel free.

"Javier." "Yes Sade?" "Did last night really happen?" Javier held out his hand for me. "Come here and look, really look. Do you see this view? Take it in, this is real. We are real. I am here Sade, and I am not leaving."

Staring over the yacht railing into the aquamarine hues of the ocean brings me clarity. "I love you Javier." "I know darling, I love you too. Now get your swimsuit on. I had the yacht salt water swimming pool filled for our trip. Let's take a dip and have breakfast by the pool." "That sounds perfect Javier. I'll be right out."

When I came out of the master suite below deck, I could hear the smooth jazz pouring from the speakers above. I walked slowly up the steps careful not to trip on my new white sheer coverup. I decided to crack my shell open a little more this morning, and let Javier know just how good it feels to be emotionally free, and to bask in the sun of unconditional love. I glided over to the pool, Javier stood up like the gentleman that he is, took my hand and helped me to sit. He had breakfast prepared and ready for us. My veggie omelet topped with feta cheese looks delicious.

We held hands while Javier led us in prayer. After breakfast was finished, we sat by the pool gazing into the deep blue waters for at least an hour. Nothing else matters right now. This is our time. I love this man. Javier leaned over and gently kissed my forehead before jumping into the water.

"Come on my love, take a swim with me." I was so relaxed and in tune with the calmness of the ocean, that I had almost forgotten Javier's morning surprise. Just thinking about it had me blushing again. But it's time we add a little naughty to this nice. I can't wait until tonight. I need it now.

"Yes, sir gladly." I stood beside the pool, and slowly pulled my coverup over my head. My eyes locked on Javier's. I could see his temperature rising.

"Sade, you are a living masterpiece. Every inch of your body is perfect to me." Javier swam toward me as I stepped into the pool. He lifted me in his arms. We made love under the sun for hours. This time it was different. It was loud, we were open and my inhibitions were set free. In his hands,

Javier now held all of me. He knew my inner most thoughts, my greatest fears and goals. He knew the silhouette of my frame, and even the touches to make my pain turn to pleasures with every stroke of love made. I opened my soul like never before. Javier is my paradise.

"Javier, you are my island, and I never want to leave." Javier reached over, picked up the bottle of champagne that had been chilling since breakfast and poured two glasses.

"Here sweetheart." Javier passed me the glass, and held his high. "Here's to our present and future. May we always remember that we are worthy of the love we pour into each other. May we always have the audacity to love out loud, no matter who has a problem with it." Javier's toast made my heart smile. We got lost in each other all over again.

After relaxing and sunbathing for a couple more hours, Javier jumped up. "Let's go shower love. I have a nice evening planned for us."

"Where are we going? What should I wear Javier?" "I am wearing my all white linen pants with the matching short sleeve top that Victoria made for me."

Javier turned and opened his garment bag.

"Sade, this is for you." Javier pulled out a beautiful salmon pink tee strapped linen sundress and handed it to me with an envelope. Tears welled in my eyes as I opened the envelope and began to read the letter inside.

Dear Sade,

Sis, I hope that you are enjoying yourself while away. Always know the children are fine and mom is too. I am happy you and Javier found home in one another. I hope this is the beginning of your true happily ever after.

I made this dress for you a while ago. Javier saw it hanging in my work studio and fell in love with it. Since I was planning to gift it to you, I decided to make him a linen outfit to compliment the dress. When I found out about the trip and was secure in how much Javier really loved you, I decided this was the perfect time to give it to you. Be happy big sister. Cherish these moments. You deserve to be loved for exactly who you are. Your scars are beautiful in their own unique way. Javier sees you. He's emptied pandora's box, yet he loves you deeper.

Sade, I am my sister's keeper. In this life and the next, I will always have your back.

I am happy for you, and I love you with all my heart and soul.

My love always, Vic

Now, with tears completely streaming down my face, I couldn't utter a word. I wrapped my arms around Javier's neck. I know it felt like I was choking him. His velvety sweet voice whispered in my ear. "I love you too Sade."

Javier walked me back towards the bed, picked me up and mounted me in my favorite seat. "After that, I am going to close my eyes for thirty minutes while you get a head start on getting ready for dinner this evening."

"Okay handsome, I promise not to attack you again. Well, not now anyway." "Woman you never need permission, I am yours whenever and wherever you need me." Smiling, I twisted my way to the shower.

Javier planned for us to have dinner at one of the best seafood restaurants in the Caribbean. He didn't give me any details other than the owner and Cher are old friends. She apparently worked with Javier and set up reservations for us.

Sitting at the vanity, I pulled out my phone to facetime Rae. "Hi Rae, how are you?" "I'm fine lady. Why are you calling me when you should be loving all over that man?" We both giggled.

"Girl I've been doing that all day, and I mean all day." "So what's up?" "I called so you can watch me get this face together for dinner tonight. Javier is taking me out for a lovely romantic dinner. Victoria made me this stunning salmon pink linen sundress for the evening, and I want my makeup to be flawless."

"Okay breathe Sade. I've taught you ladies everything I know. You can handle this. Turn the camera slightly. Great, now I can see everything. Start to transform your look. I will guide you where I think it is needed." Rae knew I could do this without her help, but having her there staring at me through the phone gave me the extra boost of confidence that I needed. I wanted a little girl time presence to remind me again that this shit is real.

"Flawless Sade, just as I expected. My dear protégé your face looks fabulous. You've taken your natural beauty and enhanced it in all the right places. Now get off this damn phone, and slip on that dress. I love you Sade, have fun!" "Thanks Rae, I love you too."

Javier hugged me from behind and spun me around. "Sade you look stunning my queen. Are you ready to go. The captain says we'll be arriving at the restaurant shortly."

"Yes, I just need to put on my shoes and grab my handbag." "You're taking the new Chanel clutch I bought you, right. "Yes love, I am."

"The clutch was a perfect color match to this dress that Victoria made for you. I was out shopping with Matthew for a gift for Cher when I saw it. I knew you'd love it. Now you know why I insisted you pack it for the trip." "You're full of surprises Javier. I can't wait to see what the rest of the night brings."

When we arrived at Angelika's Seafood and Wine Bar, personnel was there to help us from the yacht. The owner, Jonas Adderley, welcomed us and wished us a great evening. We were escorted into the restaurant to check in at the reservation desk. We were immediately escorted back outside to a private dinner cabana. Once the cabana drape was pulled, my eyes widened in shock.

"Javier, what is this?" There was a feast before me fit for kings and queens. Lobster, Crabs, Tuna steak, fresh and fried Conch, my mouth was watering from the thought of the first bite.

"Javier it's just the two of us. This looks delicious, but there's so much." Javier took my left hand, and held it gently in his. My eyes followed his as he lowered himself down onto one knee.

"Oh my God Javier, what are you doing?" "Sade, I have loved you far longer than the tenure of our relationship. You are my paradise, and I want to spend the rest of my life showing you how much I love you. Sade, will you marry me?"

"Yes! Yes, Javier I will marry you." Javier placed a perfect pear shaped three and a half karat diamond on my ring finger, and lifted me in his arms. He began spinning me around screaming at the top of his lungs.

"She said yes! She said yes!" I heard an echo after Javier took a breath. I spun my head around. It's Vic. "Surprise! Sis, did you think we would let you celebrate this moment alone. Last night and today was all the alone time you are getting for the moment. Tonight we are here to celebrate you and Javier."

"Wow Vic, I had no clue. You guys really got me." Rae gave me the biggest kiss on the cheek. "Your makeup is flawless darling." One by one they appeared. Pierre, Cher, Matthew, and Stephen all filed in one after the other.

"Well my love, now you know why there's such a feast for tonight. We are here to celebrate our engagement and who better to share in this happiness than our loved ones." "Javier, you never cease to amaze me. I appreciate you."

Pierre raised his glass and placed his arm around Javier's shoulders. "A special thanks to Stephen for flying the rest of us here safely. Now to the man of the hour, welcome to the family Javier. I couldn't be more happy for you and Sade."

This has been one of the best days of my life. What I thought was a simple getaway with the man that I love, has turned into so much more. I never thought I'd have a chance at love again, yet here I am. I said yes.

Chapter Eight

Stay

Cher

I often wonder if you can lose what you never really had. I find that the most important people in my life left me before ever getting a chance to truly know me. What was it about the possibility of knowing me that frightened them so. From My grandfather, to my parents, and even my first love, Sebastian, they all left before seeing me blossom.

I spent years crying and wondering why or how someone could walk away from a child they created. How does one find the cowardness to turn and never look back. I comprehend nor understand such selfishness. Therapy never cracked that shell.

Sure, I know it's their loss, but does no one see that I lost too. Yes, over time I've learned that darkness looms at the core of my family's history. The alternative was no picnic. I was given away at birth to be pummeled by the state. Foster care madness, being tossed from home to home as property clouds my memories. Being used to pay rent, and fulfill the selfish needs and desires of adults, built the foundation for my lack of trust. I was a paycheck. I hated it.

The foster care system is supposed to protect children, yet the majority of us were tossed around from one unloving, intolerable and abusive household to another. Most times I felt voiceless. And now, I am scared. Years later, I am terrified of losing the man that I have shared my soul with transparently. Oh yes, I believe Mathew loves me, but still my heart races in fear of the day he does what all the other men have since conception. Leave.

I love waking up to watching Matthew workout through the glass walls that surround our home gym. He's so disciplined it keeps me motivated to work out. I usually work out in the evenings before he makes it back in from work.

We flew back in last night after Javier and Sade's dinner. I am so happy for them. I felt a little insecure when everyone started throwing hints towards Matthew about popping the question. Matthew handled himself like a politician, and moved through the hints and inuendo smoothly.

This morning I find myself all jittery. No one has ever treated me as good as Matthew does. No one has ever believed in me like Matthew has, yet still I wait in fear of the day he may walk away.

Before I knew it my tea was spilling over the side of my cup. So lost in thought, I didn't realize Matthew had stopped working out, and was staring at me through the glass. He mouthed good morning to me. I giggled and blew him a kiss.

"Hey you, snap out of it. What has you so preoccupied this morning?" "It's nothing Matthew." "Oh it's something alright. You tossed and turned all night, and I know you were awake when I got up for my workout. I chose not to bother you. I figured you'd come in and talk to me when you got out of bed. Talk to me Cher."

"Last night, were you uncomfortable when the guys kept hinting about marriage?" I tried to gauge Matthew's eyes for sincerity. "Why would I be uncomfortable Cher? Why would that have you tossing and turning like a madwoman?"

"Matthew." "Yes, Cher." "I'm scared of losing you." "Where is all of this coming from Cher. I'm not going anywhere. Why would you even consider such a thing. What have I done to make you think I would ever leave?"

"Nothing. It's the insecurities in my head that cause this thinking. You haven't done anything. It's all me."

"Cher, I spend every waking moment thinking about how to support and protect you. I live to see you happy and prospering. I am inspired by your independence and ability to persevere. You are my phoenix Cher. I thrive when you rise. You are mine for a lifetime."

"I love you, and I believe you. My heart still breaks when I think of how easy it was for my parents and grandfather to leave me at birth. Then, I think about Sebastian and the pain deepens."

Tears began to fall from my eyes like the raging Nile. "Cher, stop." Wiping the tears from my cheeks Matthew picked me up and carried me to our bed. "Lay here, and please listen to me. I am not your father or your grandfather. I'm damn sure not Sebastian's ass. We have been completely open with one another about our pasts and our lives. I have lived with you through the severest of storms and your greatest triumphs."

"I know Matthew, but." "No, but nothing Cher. I said listen." "Okay, I'm listening Matthew."

"You are my world woman. I would die if it meant saving you. Please never doubt my love or loyalty to you or to our relationship."

The melody of the rain drops hitting the skylight above our bed calmed my nerves. I stood up in front of Matthew, moved in closer and straddled him. Holding me close I could see our story written in his eyes.

"Matthew have you ever thought about getting married. I mean to me. Have you thought about us getting married?" Matthew picked me up off his lap and stood me up. He got up, moved passed me and went into the closet. Right on his heels, I was curious as to what could be so important right now. Matthew opened his safe, and turned around to face me. He held a little red velvet jewelry box in his hand. Before opening it he handed me the receipt folded just so. I could only read the date of purchase, but not the price of whatever was in the box. When Matthew opened the box he dropped down on one knee. Shock riddled my body. My knees were so weak I dropped down in front of him.

"Matthew." He interrupted me. "So you asked me if I have thought about us getting married. Yes Cher, I have. I purchased this engagement ring nine months ago. I knew you weren't ready for marriage, and I refused to rush you."

"I tried so hard not to show you my insecurities Matthew." "Baby girl, your energy runs through me. I know you better than you know yourself. I can feel your fears. I don't indulge in them. I do all that I can to counteract them with my actions. You are worthy of unconditional loyalty and love, and I intend to give it to you until my dying breath."

Both kneeling before one another, Matthew held my hands in his and kissed each one. "Cher, will you make me the happiest man in the universe. Will you please do me the honor of being my wife?" "Yes, Matthew, I will."

I said yes before I could breathe my next breath. For the first time since we moved into our place on Fisher Island, we christened the closet.

Famished, from today's emotional journey, I whipped up one of Matthew's favorite meals. Homemade baked ziti and garlic bread with a side antipasto salad.

"It smells scrumptious, what a perfect close to our day. Can I call the fellas after dinner to tell them the news? Do you mind?" "Of course you can Matthew." I could barely get the words out without bursting into laughter.

"Ah, you already called Rae, Vic and Sade. You told them didn't you?" "Yes, sir, I am guilty." "I knew it. I can't wait till after dinner. I'm calling the fellas on facetime now. Get those hips over here."

"Okay baby, but let me get this off my chest first." "Sure Cher, what is it?" "Matthew, I have longed for this moment forever. I was afraid you wouldn't find me to be enough to fulfill all your needs. Although these were thoughts I created in my mind which didn't reflect your actions, I still had them. Only I have the power to banish them. You have been a king to me through and through. I don't want to imagine my world without you. I can't imagine my world without you. No matter what, please never doubt how deeply I love you."

"I love you Cher. We are one." Matthew pressed send on his call, and one by one the fellas appeared. Matthew motioned for me to come closer. He held my hand in front of the camera, showing off my four karat natural ruby diamond encrusted engagement ring.

The congratulations poured in. The guys were so excited. Pierre was all smiles. I heard Vic in the background screaming, *"I'm so excited, and I just can't hide it."* Then Rae popped up behind Stephen's head and continued Vic's song. *"I'm about to lose control and I think I like it.*

Stephen and I love you and Matthew dearly. We have so much to celebrate. See you two love birds soon." "We love you too Rae. We love each of you."

My heart is full. Javier and Sade had their faces smushed together in the camera screaming congratulations. It's too cute.

Matthew nodded at the fellas. "Guys night out coming real soon!"

Chapter Nine
Madness Falls

Victoria

It's a beautiful day to lay out by the pool. I adore Florida weather. Minus hurricane season, it's paradise. I can't wait till the crew arrives. We have some serious madness to discuss today. Lifelong secrets are on the table.

"Pierre, I'm going to take a swim and lay out by the pool. Buzz me when everyone arrives. Lunch is chilling in the refrigerator behind the bar if you want an early taste." I had fresh seafood catered. "Okay Vic, I will join you soon."

After only ten laps, I found myself laying under the gorgeous Florida sun. I opened my eyes to hellos from my people.

"Hey, hey, hey, my lovelies, how is everyone today. I hope you brought your suits, because it's one of those days. Lunch is chilling in the fridge behind the bar. Let me run and put out our spread. I'll get everyone's drinks flowing, and we can catch up."

Rae and Cher were the first to change and dive into the pool. Matthew and Stephen were right behind them.

"Sade, you look radiant today. How are you feeling? How's engagement life treating you?"

"Vic, you're so silly. Engagement life is great. Javier is amazing, but you already know this."

"I'm happy you're happy Sade. You deserve it." "Thanks Vic."

"This lobster salad is delicious Vic. We will have to talk about the recipe." That means a lot coming from my favorite chef. "Thanks Cher, I'd love to see how we can tweak it to make it even better."

"Family, I am glad you're all here, but we need to take time out to get down to the real reason we needed to come together so urgently. Now that the mood is loosened slightly, we need to dive in head first."

"Alright, Victoria, let's dive." Javier spoke with conviction. "There's no elegant way to say it. Let's just rip the bandage off without fear. I am the person that killed Sade's rapist in action. I am sure you have all pulled that much together. I really don't want to discuss it. The only reason I am bringing this up now is because I feel I don't have a choice. I am being stalked by some bastard claiming to be Theodore's son."

"Theodore, the asshole that raped Sade as a child." Pierre clarified to make sure everyone was following me. "Thanks baby." All eyes were fixated on me. The silence surrounding me was deafening.

I continued, "I have been having nightmares, and reliving the night over and over. We did not know that Theodore had children, but this person is claiming to be his son. After much digging, I was able to find out that Theodore the sequel does exist, and that he spent part of his life in a mental institution."

"A mental institution? Did he escape? Was he released? What was his diagnosis?" Rae blurted out question after question. Looking at her, I was hoping my eyes could cool the questions burning her tongue.

"Yes, a mental institution. He was committed after killing his baby sister. At the time of her death he was eight years old, and his sister only two years old."

Pierre interjected, "To answer Rae's question, yes, he escaped from Falcon Mental Institution, located in Phoenix, North Dakota."

My chest was heaving as I was practicing my breathing techniques. I need to continue. I can do this. Pierre nodded at me to keep talking.

"According to his medical records, he intentionally killed his sister because his parents showed her too much attention and favoritism. His narcissistic behavior started at a young age and grew aggressively."

Tears started pouring down my cheeks uncontrollably. I only ever wanted to keep this nightmare in the past, buried deep. Why now? And he claims to have seen the murder in progress. This means he was watching the rape, yet did nothing. Oh my goodness, he was just watching. My face began to feel numb. Pierre knew when to back off. He didn't dare wipe these tears away. Pierre let me have my moment and took over for me.

"It seems Victoria is his sole purpose for escaping the mental institution. He told her he lives to avenge his father's death. He is claiming to be the only witness that can convict Victoria of the murder. He would rather kill her himself, or so he said. He thinks we won't go to the police because of the simple fact that he's telling the truth. Vic did kill Theodore."

"She killed him in self-defense." The heartache and anger permeated through Cher's voice. "True Cher, it was in self-defense, but of me. My baby sister was protecting me. She killed him in cold blood, and we walked away as if it never happened. We buried those wounds so deep, hoping never to have them unearthed. I love you always Vic, you saved me."

"I know you love me big sis, and I would do it again if I had to. The nightmares never cease. Days just continue to accumulate as moonlight turns to sunlight again and again. Somehow we always managed to keep going. For as long as I have breath, I am my sister's keeper. I love you too, Sade."

Pierre pulled the guys aside to fill them in on the details of the harassment. "He's been calling a few times a week consistently for over a month. He hasn't demanded money or anything material. He repeats his count of the night of his father's murder. He also makes sure to remind Vic of his vow to avenge his father's death when we least expect it."

Javier began to pace. "We need to get surveillance and other security measures around here heightened." "I agree, Javier, I already have. I will walk you through the changes I've made, and you can offer any additional recommendations."

"You got it brother, anything for you and Victoria." "Thank you Javier. Thank you all for always being here. Matthew and Stephen, I am so happy for you both. Right now is such an exciting time for both of you. I hate dumping this shit in your lap now of all times."

Matthew pulled everyone in closer. "This is what brothers are for. If it hits one of us, it hits all of us. It's how we thrive. We will get this psychotic bastard, and our lives will return to celebration mode. We are here for you Pierre." Matthew felt and meant every word.

"I feel as if his eyes are watching my every move. I constantly feel like I am being followed. This creature from hell has me paranoid. He is jeopardizing the safety of my loved ones. Being in my presence puts your safety at risk."

"Nonsense Vic. I don't give a flying fuck about my safety being at risk. You are our sister! I wish we knew sooner the magnitude of what you were going through." Rae was furious. Her breathing started to quicken.

"Me too Rae, but that doesn't matter." Cher tried to speak in a calming tone. She put her arm around Rae's shoulder to ease her anxiousness.

"All that matters is that we know now, and we are here to fight. Rae, Sade and I will fight with you Victoria until this prick is dead or back in a mental institution." "I appreciate you Cher, I am grateful for all of you."

Pierre played the recordings of our harassment calls. "After the first call, I began recording my phone calls for safety reasons. We were able to trace his location from the last call made to a warehouse in Ocean Harbor. By the time Pierre arrived, the warehouse had been abandoned."

"Pierre went alone Vic?" "Yes, Sade, he didn't want to involve anyone else unless absolutely necessary. He was trying to protect everyone."

"I can't help but feel that this is all my fault. If I hadn't been raped and abused by Theodore, his son never would have been there to witness Vic saving my life. I am he reason he witnessed his father's murder." "Shut that shit up Sade. I will never let you take the blame for what that creep did to you, and I don't care about the consequences. I would shoot that motherfucker again and again a thousand times. He had no right to rape you of your innocence. Don't ever apologize for him getting what he deserved." I feel a migraine coming on. My sweet big sister has to know that I would never let anyone take advantage of her and get away with it. She knows I'm a warrior sprit.

"Victoria is right Sade. Don't feel guilty for what he did to you! You did not deserve it, and you are not to blame for his son harassing my wife. Your sister doesn't blame you. No one here blames you. You have to stop blaming yourself. I am your brother-in-law. If anything bothers you or Vic, it bothers me. I'm honored to have a wife that would protect her family at all costs. We wouldn't have it any other way Sade."

"Pierre's right my love. You have to stop blaming yourself." Javier pulled Sade close and held on for dear life.

Pierre's militant tone echoed through the room, interrupting the conversations in my head. "I put a great deal of thought into our plan. I think the best way to keep Victoria safe is to get her out of the house. I believe the house is under twenty-four hour video surveillance. To be safe, we will sneak her out in the trunk of the range rover. There were too many specifics dropped in real time during the last call. If his pattern stays the same, his next call is set for tomorrow night at 9:06 sharp."

"So what about the rest of us Pierre?"
I could tell Rae was growing impatient. It's hard for her to sit still while she's in protection mode. "Rae, Matthew is going to get you and the ladies set up at his house today. Cher is going to take you to Fisher Island until further notice. You all are going to stay there together."

"Matthew, Javier, Stephen and I are going to stay here. We will let you know when it's safe to return to the mainland. You will already be on the island when tomorrow night's call comes in. Javier has had the calls rerouted so that you don't miss it.

We will be on the line with you. Remember to keep him on the call as long as possible to help us trace his current location. We will find him."

I grabbed Pierre's hand and kissed it tenderly. "I hope so." "It seems like only yesterday we were finally through the Antonio-Joshua situation and now this. The past is a beast trying to soak up life's beauty."

"I understand the feeling, but focus Vic. I need my wife to remain strong. When he calls the main thing is to make sure he believes you're home alone. We have arranged to remove all the cars except for yours and return to the house undetected. I have opened up the tunnel we had built when we first moved in. This way, we will be able to move about accordingly when necessary."

"Please be careful Pierre. I love you." "I love you too Vic; we will."

Chapter Ten

Face to Face

Javier

It's horrifying to think of what Theodore did to my woman. He took advantage of her vulnerabilities. He caused her to spend years feeling ashamed of his actions. She felt tainted and unclean no matter how hard she scrubbed and exfoliated. I've spent hours listening to the silent cries, and seeing her try to scrub him from her memory shower after shower. I wish I could cleanse her of his existence and presence. No matter what I do, he creeps in. Now it's through his son, TJ. I can't believe there is two of them.

"Good morning Javier." "It's morning Matthew, I just don't know how good it is." "I hear you brother; Pierre and Stephen are on their way downstairs."

"Fellas, come in the kitchen, let's sit at the table and have breakfast while I share the plan for today." Pierre had that straight no chaser undertone in his voice. I was starving after the night I had trying to get Sade to calm down. We all filed in one behind the other. Pierre put all the food on the table, and we began to serve ourselves.

"As a recap, last night, Javier, Stephen and I checked on the home's security, while Matthew secured our arsenal. We made a few necessary changes, including activating the window blackout coverings. Now all windows will be secured. We will be able to see out, however no one will be able to see in. I had them installed over a year ago and never activated them."

The coverings will definitely come in handy, I may have to look into adding them to Sade's place.

"Pierre, I think I want to put the same blackout coverings on Sade's windows once this is over." "That's an excellent idea Javier, and I will help you." "Thanks brother." "You're welcome, Javier.

To wrap up, I have checked, cleaned and logged every weapon we have in our possession. I have set up several strategic traps throughout the landscape of the property. I expect the monster to pay us a visit within the next seventy-two hours after realizing Victoria is finally home alone. He will see this as his perfect opportunity to attack." Pierre searched our faces to make sure we were all following him.

It seems like Pierre thought of everything, or at least he tried to. "Aside from Vic's various social media posts, she will also have her car parked in the driveway to make it seem like she is at home. Her posts will brag about how relaxing her weekend is at home alone while the hubby and his friends enjoy a guys' weekend to celebrate the bachelors' pending nuptials. I'm sure he's been stalking Vic and Sade's social media for months."

"I agree Pierre, that asshole has probably been stalking all of our social media pages especially the women."

"Exactly Javier. I also checked to make sure the security cameras are all working properly. The footage is uploaded to the app I had you download on your phones. There's nothing more to be done right now, except enjoy some bourbon while we sit and wait for tonight's phone call. I've been running on adrenaline all day." Javier nodded, agreeing with Pierre, and held his glass up towards Stephen. It was his signal for Stephen to take the lead. Stephen did just that.

"Pierre is right, everyone has been running on adrenaline all day. Pilot Stephen is taking control of this flight for now. It's time to sip and breathe for a while." We all followed Stephen to as he led the way to the pool bar.

Having an indoor heated pool comes in handy in times like these. The walls are sound proof and the windows are now newly secured with special coverings. We can enjoy the moonlight without being seen. On normal days, the roof retracts and the Florida sun shines through. Matthew turned on

Pierre's play list and Wu Tang Clan took center stage. We let go for a couple hours.

"I know we can see every inch of the property on the island, I'm going to call and check on the ladies. I need to hear Rae's voice."

"Understood Stephen. When you get Rae, please tell her to have Cher turn on the audio with the surveillance system. She forgot to turn it on, and we can't hear anything otherwise." "Will do Matthew. I'm calling now."

Rae

"Rae, how are you holding up? "Hey Stephen." I nearly jumped out of my skin when the phone rang.

"Hey babe how are you and the fellas doing? Is everyone okay?" "Yes, Rae we are good. High on adrenaline, we are ready to unload." "I understand Stephen, but you all need to calm down before you explode. Also, we can see you moving around, but we can't hear anything."

"You are correct Rae. Matthew said to have Cher make sure the audio is turned on. On our end it's connected, so everything should work once Cher turns it on." "Hold on Stephen, I'll have her do it while you're on the line so you can confirm if its working properly." "Okay. How are Victoria and Sade handling everything since you arrived?" "No change. They are both mentally and emotionally drained. Vic and I just finished fighting for the heavy weight title in the gym. I was happy to oblige. I have mad steam still to blow off."

"Stay strong Rae. I need you to focus on what's most important. Your safety, and the safety of your sisters." "I understand Stephen. I know there's no time for emotional rants. That's why I put the gloves on. Cher said the audio should be working now babe."

"Is the volume working now, can you hear me?" "Yes, loud and clear Stephen." "Alright, I'm all clammy drenched in sweat. I love you Stephen. I'm going to take nice hot shower and try to calm my nerves." "I love you too Rae."

This is what I need right now. Just me and this scalding hot water beating on my back. I wish I could freeze time. I can't believe we are in this predicament. I have good news of my own to share, but with the two engagements and now this ordeal with Theodore's spawn, the timing doesn't seem right.

Oh no, not now. Really! I made it to the toilet just in time to throw up breakfast and last night's dinner. Shit, this damn morning sickness is turning into an afternoon and night thing too.

"You alright in there Rae?" "Yes, Sade I'm good. My stomach is just a little queasy, that's all." "I'll go make you a glass of ginger ale, and leave it on your nightstand." "Thanks Sade."

I don't think there is anything left in me to come out. Hopefully now I can finish my shower in peace. I just confirmed with my doctor yesterday evening that I am pregnant. I was so excited when the test results came in. I immediately started planning a surprise reveal for Stephen in my head. I wish I had just told him right away. Now I'm here and he's there. Everything spiraled so quickly. I am the only one that knows. I am so scared to bring a soul into this unforgiving world. It's still hard to wrap my brain around the fact that I am going to be someone's mother, correction, am someone's mother. Wow.

Sade's hand tapped on the door. "I put your drink on the nightstand. When you're dressed, come down stairs and sit with us." I turned the shower off and took a deep breath. "Thanks sis, I will be down soon."

I have got to pull myself together. Now is not about me. I put on my sweats, finished my ginger ale and made my way down stairs. Cher was waiting for me to sit with glass in hand.

"Bourbon and honey for the lady. Now that we are all here together, we can talk. Let's toast to perseverance and sisterhood. Salute."

"You know you have to drink with the toast Rae." Cher started giggling, winking at Sade and Victoria. "Ha. Yes, I know that Cher." "Okay then we're waiting Rae." "I can't right now Cher. My stomach is aching. I think it's my nerves. This is all so unsettling."

Sade looked at me with her puppy dog eyes and whispered, "I'm sorry sis. I saw the prenatal vitamins on the dresser when I came in to check on you. You probably forgot they were sitting out. I told them. Are you pregnant?" "Um okay. This isn't how I planned to tell anyone. It's all happening so fast. I just confirmed it yesterday evening. With your engagements and the disaster with Theodore's son, I just figured my news could wait.

Oh my God, the surveillance system is on! My Stephen!" We all turned our heads toward the camera in the room and we saw the men looking back at us. Stephen was now kneeling on floor in shock.

"Yes, Rae I hear you. Are we having a baby?"
"Yes Stephen, we are having a baby."

The girls gathered around and surrounded me in a group hug. Peace covered me until reality kicked in thanks to the phone ringing. It's 9:06 at night, it's time.

Victoria

"Hello." I tried to steady my voice so it wouldn't sound like I was panicking. "This will be my last call. The next time we talk, will be face to face. I just called to hear the fear in your vibrato. I can't wait to taste you, and spit you out to the wolves."

"You sick fuck. You're a coward. I hope you and your disgusting father rot in hell." "Oh bitch, I see you. Someone will be burning, but it won't be me."

The piercing sound of the phone slamming down shook me cold. My body started trembling. Sade grabbed me and helped to steady my breathing. My heart is racing. His last words echoed in my head. *Oh bitch, I see you. Someone will be burning, but it won't be me.*

Pierre

"Something isn't right. His tone was different with this call. He sounds far more arrogant and confident." Matthew agreed. "We've all listened to the recordings. Pierre is right, TJ seemed to have an extra edge in his tone tonight."

"I can't chance it, he said *I see you.* I can't run the risk of him meaning that literally. To be safe, I have to get to the island tonight."

"I'm with you Pierre. We can take the speedboat, its gassed up and ready to go." "Thanks Stephen." "Not a thought Pierre. Let's go."

"Pierre, I've got shit here. You know I can handle it bro. If he comes anywhere near this property I will get him. No question about it. Your home is good brother. You, Stephen and Matthew get to the island!" "Thank you Javier." "I'm on it Pierre."

"I'm ready. Let's get out of here Stephen. Javier, let Cher know we are on our way."
Cher nodded at the camera, she heard everything.

Chapter Eleven

Choices

Pierre

I will never forgive myself if anything happens to the ladies. The night sky is pitch black. There's not a star in sight. The temperature is barely cool enough to keep my anger from boiling over. I am driving this boat as fast as I can. It feels like we are moving in slow motion.

"Fuck!" "Calm down Pierre, you can't predict everything. You don't even know if TJ will come to the island. He's a psychotic dead man walking. I got your back. Try to calm your nerves before we arrive." Stephen is trying his best to calm my fury. It isn't working.

"I hear you Stephen, but I underestimated him as if I knew him. I never do that. I shouldn't have assumed anything." "Pierre there is nothing you can do about how we've come to this moment in time. What we can do is be even more vigilant moving forward."

"We will be there soon. I just couldn't live with myself if anything ever happened to them." "I know Pierre, none of us could."

When we pulled up to the doc, Vic and Cher were there to greet us. "I thought we'd never get here. I pushed this little speed boat as fast as I could. I had to get to you Vic. Until the last phone call, it hadn't dawned on me that Theodore may try to attack you from here."

Vic jumped into my arms and nestled her head in her favorite spot, just under the tip of my shoulder. "I love you baby. We need to move." "I know Pierre. I love you too. Everything is speculation. We don't know where he really is. He could still be on the mainland. I'm so glad you are here with me."

"Vic, where's Rae and Sade?" "Laying down upstairs in Cher's room. They're okay Matthew, just exhausted. We all are exhausted." Matthew headed upstairs to see for himself. Cher nodded in agreeance with Rae.

"Yeah, we are all exhausted. I told them to go upstairs and rest in my room while it was quiet. Of course I cooked for a couple hours to clear my mind. Help yourselves, I made lasagna if you're hungry." "Thanks Cher." "You're welcome Pierre."

"I hired a private security team to protect the property here on the island months ago. With us constantly coming and going, Matthew feels more secure knowing the place is monitored with additional security personnel." "Yep Cher, that sounds like my brother. I agree with him too."

"Pierre, you know how Matthew is. If I didn't, he would've done it for me. I called them in to work until further notice. I sent you pictures of each of them so you know who belongs and who doesn't." "That's perfect Cher. Have you noticed anything strange or suspicious since the phone call?" "Nothing Pierre."

Matthew is headed back downstairs. The girls must still be asleep. "Are they asleep Matthew?" "Yes Pierre, they are both still knocked out. Are you ready to do a sweep of the property?" "Yes sir. I'm with you Matthew."

We grabbed some lasagna from the island in the kitchen and scarfed it down. Matthew and I did a thorough sweep of the property. We checked every inch multiple times before coming back inside. When we returned, Rae and Sade were sitting at the kitchen island bar talking to Cher and Vic.

"Matthew and I didn't notice anything out of the ordinary." I tried to speak in a reassuring tone, but my nerves are shot. Just as the thought lingered in my head, we all heard a loud banging sound coming from the front of the house. Matthew motioned for the girls to stay in the kitchen, while he and Stephen went to check it out. The security guards didn't see anything but they heard the banging too. We did another sweep of the property. The flood lights lit up the night sky. I walked around towards the dock again. Just as I was passing Stephen's speedboat I heard a faint thud that came from the Bourbon Princess. I sent Matthew a text.

I heard something coming from the Bourbon Princess. Get back here man, I'm going aboard to check it out.

Matthew rushed back into the house. "Stephen is right outside the door. Ladies, I need you to watch the security cameras on the dock and yacht. Keep your eyes glued to the camera. Cher, text if you see anything coming my way." "On it Matt."

There it is again. This time it sounds more like a faint thud. I'm prepared to shoot the first thing that moves. I turned back for a second, and I could see Matthew heading down the dock toward me. There were a couple of security guards behind him. I motioning for them to hurry. I stepped on board, lifted the latch for the door to the lower deck and pulled it open. I began to walk down the stairs. It's where the sound seemed to be coming from. As I stepped down from the last step, I heard the door above shut. I turned around to see a bomb strapped to the chest of a strange man. He stood just over six feet tall and had dark deceptive eyes.

He looked exactly like the picture of his father, Theodore.

"I know who you are. You look exactly like your father. That monster tortured my sister-in-law, and now you think you can torture my wife for protecting her sister all those years ago."
I lifted my gun standing at point blank range. I pulled out my phone and sent Matthew a text.

> *Stand down. Call the detective back and let him know Theodore is definitely here. He has a bomb strapped to his body. Get back to the house and get the ladies into a secure area. Fill in Javier and Stephen.*

A look of shock masked Matthew's face.

> *Shit! Security checked the yacht and this property extensively before the ladies came. I saw to it. This is fucked up. Okay bro, got it.*

"Alright it's just me and you. What is your plan exactly? I'll never let you close to Victoria or any of us again." "Pierre you don't control shit. Yeah, I know who you are. There won't be time to diffuse the bomb. I will have my justice. Right here, right now. You being here is the greatest gift I could have hoped for."

"TJ, how could you stand by and watch your father rape Sade all those years ago?" "She was my savior you idiot. When she came along, I no longer had to endure the sexual abuse from that monster anymore. Sade freed me. My father became so fixated on Sade that he began to sodomize and torture me less."

"To be clear, in your twisted mind you think it is justified as long as the abuse stopped happening to you. I still don't get it. When Victoria killed your father, why didn't you consider yourself free of the pain he inflicted. Why would you hold a grudge with the woman that freed you from his brutality?" "He was all I had Pierre. Sade and Victoria moved on and managed to make a decent life for themselves. I was stuck with therapy and the memories of my father's transgressions. With him not here to blame, somehow I rationalized blaming Victoria for killing him. She has been the object of my obsession ever since."

I looked him square in the eyes and saw nothing there. TJ was an empty shell staring back at me. I glanced at the timer on the bomb and again at the door above. There was less than a minute left on the timer.

"Don't think about it. Once the door closed behind you, a trigger was set. The bomb is rigged to go off immediately if anyone opens that door again. You will die with me, and no one can save you." TJ waved at the camera as if he knew Victoria was watching.

"Killing you is far sweeter revenge than killing Victoria. By taking the love of her life away, she will agonize without you daily. Her mind will live in torture, wondering what she could have done differently. She will blame herself for your death."

"You're sick! I'm not dying with you, I'll take the satisfaction of killing you first." I pulled the trigger and the gun jammed. Fuck! I tried again. Nothing. I bent down and pulled the piece out of my ankle holster and shot.
TJ fell to the floor. I could not hear them, but I could see the mouths on the video screen telling me to get off the boat.

Matthew

Everything is happening so fast. Come on Pierre get the hell out of there. The house is swarming with law enforcement. The bomb squad just arrived. Victoria came running down the dock. I scooped her up in one full-swoop.
"Hold on sis, I can't let you go. We know Pierre shot Theodore, but the bomb is still active."

"I need my man Matthew." With tears streaming down her face, Vic began to plead. "Please Matthew, I need Pierre." "Vic, I promised Pierre above all else that I would keep you safe. I can't let you go."

Walking back towards the house, I lowered Vic down onto her feet. Immediately she took off toward the yacht. Just as I got close enough to snag her shirt tail and pull her in, there was an earth shattering explosion. The Bourbon Princess was blown into a million pieces right before our eyes. Debris was flying everywhere. Sade, Rae and Cher came running from the house. Our eyes locked on the blinding sea of fire that filled the sky. It was like a scene from a movie. Victoria's screams resounded continuously. Pierre and TJ are dead. Sade, Rae and Cher hovered over Vic, picked her up and carried her to the house. We were all in shock.

Chapter Twelve

Alone

Victoria

It's been one month, two days, twelve hours and counting since Pierre's memorial service. Pierre wanted to be cremated. It broke my heart all over again when I learned that the authorities weren't able to find his body after the explosion. They think he went overboard in the explosion. It was a quiet homegoing ceremony with our immediate circle of family and friends. I rented a yacht for the service. We anchored in the middle of the Atlantic just south of Key West. It's where he wanted his ashes scattered. I wasn't able to do that for him, but at least I could be in his favorite place, at sea.

I have no desire to be around anyone. The messages from the girls are piling up. Sade creeps into my house every other day to check on me. We don't talk. I let her see me, and then she leaves. I feel nothing but numbness. I know Sade only wants to help, but no one can help. I just need time alone. She and Javier asked me to move in with them multiple times. I haven't responded. If Sade didn't drop off food from Cher a few times a week, I wouldn't be eating. I haven't left my house since I locked the door behind me following Pierre's homegoing celebration. I have nothing to give the rest of the world. I know Sade has mom with her.

The two of them can take care of each other. I can't stay here, and I can't move in with Javier and Sade right now. I need space and time to think and breathe. I never imagined a future without Pierre. I have to go somewhere where no one knows my name. I must get away from the monotony that is my life.

Before I could think, I purchased a first class one-way ticket to Las Vegas. Then I booked the presidential suite at the Aria Hotel. I paid upfront for a month. For once in my life I was not going to commit to someone's timeline. My stay is indefinite. I can design from anywhere, except this home that I shared with Pierre. Nothing will ever be the same. By the time Sade makes it here tomorrow, I'll already be in Las Vegas. I'll leave her a note on my refrigerator. She'll see it when she puts the food up. Sade can fill in Javier, Matthew and the girls. I finished off the last of my steak marsala leftovers and cleaned up the kitchen. Now it's time to go upstairs to pack.

Dragging my luggage downstairs, I remembered our stash. I carefully wrapped two bottles of my unopened moonshine. I started distilling my own whiskey three years ago. No one knew but me and Pierre. He was supposed to taste this first batch with me. Now, I must go at it alone.

By the time I made it to the airport I could only think about putting my feet up, plugging my earphones in and sipping some whiskey all the way to Vegas. I made it through security and found my gate. I had almost an hour until my flight was ready to take off. I walked over to the Flamingo Bar and Grill just across the way and settled in at the bar. Why should I wait? I might as well start this party for one now. Thanks to the bartender, the hour flew by. His witty sarcasm and conversation was right on time. I took my last old fashioned to go and nestled into my first class seat. This plane can't take off fast enough.

TJ hadn't shared his knowledge of my criminal acts with anyone. His obsession to seek revenge caused him to keep the truth he knew hidden. The investigation was open and shut. I have a chance to try to regain control of my life, and find a way to move forward. That's exactly what I plan to do. I am a widow. My husband was murdered at the hands of my actions. I will live with this truth until my dying breath.

"Hello, my name is Victor, your flight attendant. May I get you something to drink ma'am?" "Yes please. I'll have a double shot of tequila. I have a lot of forgetting to do."

Victor winked at me and returned with my drink right away. "Thank you Victor, my name is Victoria." "Cheers Victoria, you're very welcome."

After Victor served the other three people in first class, he talked to me about the best places to dine, and the must see shows in Las Vegas. We hit it off and exchanged contact information. It was a breath of fresh air to have frivolous conversation with someone who didn't know about my past or my pain.

Victor is from Vegas and will be home on vacation for a few weeks. I was gifted an open invitation to hit him up if I wanted to hang out together. I threw the ball in his court and told him to give me a call when the mood hits him.

I don't remember drifting off to sleep, but the sound of the pilot telling us to prepare for landing woke me up. I slept like a baby. I got my thoughts together and gathered my belongings. I was ready to get to my hotel and enjoy a long, hot shower. As I was exiting the plane, I felt a tap on my arm.

"I'll talk to you soon Victoria, and remember, what happens in Vegas stays in Vegas." I could tell Victor would definitely be a good time if nothing else. That's what I wanted, a good time in a different world. I just want to forget about the last thirty years of my life. Wiping the slate clean and starting anew sounds inviting.

My smile grew brighter thinking about Victor.

"What happens in Vegas stays in Vegas".

I caught an uber from the airport to my hotel. Good, there's no line. Checking in should be quick. As expected, within a couple of minutes I'm handed my room keys and welcome envelope. My suite was heavenly. The first thing I noticed was the hot tub in front of the balcony doors overlooking the strip.

I ordered a bottle of champagne, filet mignon and two slices of Crown Royal Peach pound cake. I couldn't strip out of my clothes fast enough. I turned the shower on and stared at my naked reflection in the mirror until the steam blocked my view. As soon as I stepped into the shower my phone rang. I ignored it. Whoever it is can leave a message. This shower is everything. I let the water beat down on my back. It helped to loosen the tension flowing through my veins.

I turned the water to cold before getting out of the shower and let my pores awaken. I felt refreshed. My new swim suit was laid out on the bed. Designed by me for me, I slid into my firetruck red one piece halter swim suit. I turned the hot tub on and opened the blinds so I could enjoy the view. Once my dinner arrives, I will eat, drink, soak and let the night lead me where it may.

The Vegas sun kissed my cheeks awakening me out of an amazing sleep. For the first time in a long time I felt rested. Everyone is so concerned about my abrupt decision to leave town. Grieving the loss of the man I thought I'd grow old and enjoy grandchildren with has been devasting. I can't just sit around our home and travel through our city knowing that I am traveling alone. A change of scenery was necessary to fuel the creativity in my soul.

Pierre always reminded me that I didn't owe anyone an explanation regarding the decisions I choose to make for my life. That's one of the most valuable lessons I learned from Pierre. It helped me to make the decision to take an extended vacation and clear my head.

The sound of windchimes filled the room. I loved the doorbell here. Hopefully that's room service, because I'm starving. "Good morning ma'am, my name is Vanessa. Where would you like for me to put your breakfast?" "Good morning, I'm Victoria. You may place it on the dining room table. Thank you Vanessa." "You're welcome ma'am."

I finished my veggie omelet in five minutes flat. It was delicious, and the apple smoked pineapple chicken sausage is simply addictive. I am ready to get out of this room and soak up some fresh air.

My first stop of course must be Caesar's Palace. There's a Mont Blanc store there just calling my name. I can't wait to get the new apple green diamond and ruby encrusted pen. I placed my order online, and requested it be gift wrapped. It's a gift to me from Pierre. He used to buy me a pen every year knowing that my writing is always put on the back burner when it comes to the many hats I wear. Now I will keep up the tradition. I'll buy myself a new pen every year like Pierre did as a beautiful reminder of how much he supported all of my creative dreams.

"Good day and welcome to Mont Blanc Las Vegas." "Good day, I am here to pick up my order." "Yes ma'am, your name?" "Queen Victoria." The clerk looked up at me with a puzzled look.

"Is there a problem sir?" "No Queen Victoria, your order is gift wrapped and ready." "Thank you sir, have a marvelous day."

You would have thought I just won the lottery the way I was smiling. I loved my pens and my journals. After Pierre passed I started writing in my journal again. It's been very therapeutic to write void of biased eyes.

I have raided the stores in Caesar's Palace, the Bellagio and the Venetian. Now I am going to head over to the Wynn Las Vegas and check out the commercial space I will be leasing for my Las Vegas Artistry boutique.

I meet Damion for dinner at eight o'clock to finalize the details. Pierre and I found him together once we decided that Las Vegas would be the third location for the new shop. I didn't have the strength to call and tell him that Pierre was killed. I emailed him instead, and assured him that once I was ready, I was still moving forward with my plans.

I'm ready damnit! It's all so exciting. This will be location number three. I have one in Coral Gables, on Fisher Island, and now I will add Las Vegas to the Artistry family. Pierre and I were looking at properties for the third store over the last four months. We just hadn't gotten the opportunity to move forward.

The Wynn Las Vegas space was our favorite of all the possibilities. I decided to make a decision and go for it. Pierre's passing reminded me that tomorrow is not promised.

Dinner tonight should be phenomenal. I've seen and heard amazing reviews about the cuisine at Amor Steakhouse, Las Vegas. Just thinking about it has my mouth watering.

It's five o'clock already. The elevator attendant was about to shut the doors when he saw me approaching. I added a light jog to my step. I hate to hold up others. "Please hold the elevator sir." "Of course ma'am, it's a lovely afternoon for a swim." "Yes indeed. I've been out shopping all day. I want to hurry up and enjoy the pool before the sun sets." "Enjoy your stay ma'am." "Thank you sir, I intend to. Thanks for holding the elevator."

I was in my room and changed in a flash. My body is ready to get down to the pool for a nice swim, and a glass of bourbon before I have to get ready for dinner.

I noticed the light blinking on my phone. I'm pretty sure the messages are from the girls. I need a few days, I'll call them soon. Right now, I just need to separate myself from all that reminds me of home.

It's time for this skin to be kissed by the sun. Summer is my favorite season of the year. Of course being a Leo makes me biased. Las Vegas is a melting pot during the summer months, and fades into a weather oasis in autumn. Winters in Vegas leave the heart in a picture perfect wonderland, compliments of the stunning snowcapped mountains.

"A double shot of Angel's Envy neat please." "Coming right up." "Oh wow, this is a triple, what do I owe you." "Nothing at all Victoria. Your sister called the front desk this morning and gave us strict orders to charge her credit card for all of your dining and cocktail needs." "She did what?" "Yes Victoria, your sister told us you prefer to be called by your first name only, and she made sure we had the bar stocked with your favorite whiskey and bourbon." "I had no idea. Wow."
Sade never ceases to amaze me

"The assistant manager spoke with your sister this morning. Sounds like she just wanted to do something nice for you, and let you know you're not alone even when you think you are."
Sade never ceases to amaze me. She knows me like the back of her hand. "Well sir, thank you for filling me in on the tea. I appreciate the triple shot. I know everything is paid for so here's an additional twenty-five dollars for your tip jar."

After a couple hours melting in this summer sun, it's time to shower and get ready for dinner. I'm feeling nice thanks to my sweet Sade.

Chapter Thirteen

Picking up the Pieces

Sade

I know my sister needs space. I get it, but it's not like Vic to ignore my calls. Last night, I ended up calling the front desk at the Aria to confirm that she arrived in Las Vegas safely. She didn't call or text me back. She said she needed this time and space to heal and create away from all the memories.

Javier invited Rae and Stephen over for dinner tonight. Matthew and Cher won't be able to make it. They are on the island trying to regain some sense of normalcy. We all are seeking peace and nights void of terrifying dreams.

Javier grilled mahi and vegetables. I made my famous guacamole and salsa for our lime tortilla chips and cracked open a bottle of bourbon.

Rae and Stephen let themselves in and found us out back. "Grab yourselves a glass before you sit down. I left them chilling in the freezer behind the pool bar. The bourbon is here on the table." "Thanks Sade, Bourbon will get you everything," Stephen quipped. "Ha! Okay smarty pants, you're welcome." Stephen knew how to lighten the mood. He and Rae are a perfect balance for each other.

Rae came over and sat next to me. I know you are constantly craving apple juice. I made you a fresh jar of my homemade apple juice this morning. I'll run and grab it for you. It will taste great in your chilled glass."

"I'll get it Sade. I have to go inside to get another pan anyway." "Thanks Javier, it's on the second shelf in the door of the refrigerator."

Rae smiled. "Thanks Sade, I appreciate you." "Of course, how are you feeling these days." "The morning sickness is happening less which is great. According to the doctor the baby is healthy thus far. We brought pictures of our sonogram to show you and Javier." "Ahh how cute Rae, I can't wait to see them." "The pictures will melt your heart."

"How are the twins? How's mom doing? Are they home?" "The twins are doing well. I do my best to shield them from the turmoil our family has been through. They are upstairs sleeping with mom. She's resting and binge watching her Netflix shows. You can run up and say hello if you want. She asks about you all the time."

"I love mama Sophia so much Sade. I'm going up to hug and kiss up on her and the twins. I'll be right back down for dinner." "Girl take your time. I'll get the door for you. I'll be outside with the guys."

"Sade, can you grab the steaks from the refrigerator, I am ready to throw them on the grill."

"Sure Javier, do you need anything else while I'm up?" Javier leaned down and kissed me on my forehead. "We're good for now sweetheart."

I've been marinating the steaks since yesterday afternoon. They are going to taste so good. I can't wait to eat.

I know the fellas have just as much catching up to do as Rae and I do. We've all been in a whirlwind since everything happened with TJ and Pierre being killed. Victoria is so distant now, and something other than mourning the loss of Pierre is going on with Cher and Matthew.

"I'm taking another dip in the pool until Rae comes back down. Let me know if you handsome gentleman need anything." "Thanks Sade." "You're at home Stephen, you know this. Whatever you need, we got you."

I swam a few laps. When I came up for air, Rae was walking up. "Oh my goodness Sade, I can't believe how fast the children are growing. Mom looks good considering everything that's happened." "Girl those children eat like their momma, and they are busybodies like their Aunt Vic. Especially Lea, I swear I was just the surrogate and she's Vic's child. It's crazy how much she reminds me of my sister. It helps a little actually, because I miss Vic so much."

"I miss her too Sade, but we have to give her the space she needs to heal, regroup and move forward. I don't blame her for wanting to get away from it all." Rae spoke with a softened tone, trying to ease my nerves.

"I called the hotel to at least find out if she made it to town safely. I called back a couple hours later pretending to be Vic to confirm the checkout date." I was shocked, to say the least, when I found out how long she reserved her suite for." "Well Sade, how long did she reserve her suite for?" "She booked the presidential suite at the Aria for a month. She is not returning anytime soon."

"A month! Okay wow, I didn't think Vic would be gone that long. Your sister can definitely take care of herself. Let's see how communicative she is over the next couple of weeks. Give her a little time. If necessary, we can hop on a flight and pop up to check on her. For now, we wait."
"I know you're right Rae. I just worry about her. She's always going to be my little sister."

"The food is ready ladies." Javier's words were music to Rae's ears. "Finally Javier, I'm starving." We all laughed at Rae. The distraction was needed. "I'm eating for two. That's my excuse, and I'm sticking to it. I'll have extra of everything."

Stephen made Rae's plate. "Sweetness, you always eat extra of everything, baby or no baby. That's why I love cooking for you."

Mahi, steak, asparagus, mushrooms, peppers and parmesan mashed potatoes, everything looks delicious. A man that can cook has always been sexy to me. Javier throws down in the kitchen, and he is a whiz with his homemade seasonings and marinades. He genuinely enjoys cooking which adds extra love to his food.

Stephen held up his glass to give a toast. "Here's to Sade and Javier. Congratulations again on your engagement, and thank you for having us over for another fire feast. Cheers."

"Thanks man, Sade and I would like to toast to you and Rae also. Congratulations on your bundle of joy. We couldn't be happier for you. Leo and Lea will finally have a little cousin to take care of and boss around. Salute."

Our stomachs are full. I am ready to chill. "Please excuse us gentleman, Rae and I need a little girl time." We sauntered over to the jacuzzi. I got in and let the heat soothe my body. Rae sat on the side and put her feet in. Stephen refreshed our drinks and brought them over to us.

"Here are your drinks ladies, enjoy. I'm about to go beat up on your man Sade." "Don't hurt him too bad Stephen." The two of them will be on the pool table for hours. It feels good to see them relaxing for a change.

"Alright Javier it's time to open up a can of whoop ass on you. Rack em' up. Loser treats the winner and his woman to dinner at the restaurant of the winner's choosing." "You're on Stephen!"

Rae and I showered and changed. I started the fire in the living room and warmed up some of momma's sweet potato pie. We were sitting under the fire enjoying our pie and girl talk when the men came in from shooting pool.

"Who won?" "You already know Sade. I cleaned house on your man."

"It's all good. You got me this time. I'll make good on my bet." Stephen cleared his throat. "I know you will Javier, and I'm looking forward to it."

"Honey if there is food involved, Stephen is coming to win all day every day. My man loves to eat. You all know this. I keep telling him he better be careful. He's going to end up gaining the same amount of baby weight as I am if he doesn't watch it." Rae laughed knowing what Stephen was going to say. "Kiss me woman! I keep telling you, my solution is to simply work out more during the pregnancy. I have food cravings too, and I am not depriving myself." Stephen sat down on the pillow behind Rae, pulling her in closer between his legs. It was adorable to see him rubbing her belly. Javier brought us over more sweet potato pie and sat with us.

"Sade, how many days are you going to give Vic before you try reaching out to her again?" "I don't know Stephen. I was talking to Rae about it earlier. We agree we should give her a little time to be quiet and do her. If she doesn't open the lines of communication within the next couple of weeks, then I will decide what to do next."

"I understand Sade. Remember, Rae and I are here to support you, whatever you need. If I have to fly us to Vegas for a pop up visit, I will. All you have to do is say the word." "I appreciate you Stephen. I will."

"On another note, Javier and I were talking earlier this week about your baby shower. We were so honored when you asked us to be the Godparents. Please let us host your baby shower. We can keep it intimate. I know how you are Rae. You have to let us celebrate you." Rae leaned over and hugged me. "Thanks sis, I love you."
"Is that a yes?" "Yes, it is Sade," Rae responded blushing and smiling from ear to ear.

"Awesome. I already spoke to Grace. We will host it at our new beachfront seafood bar. The business will be open by then."

"Listen Stephen, you and Rae should just stay here tonight. Take one of the guest rooms. I'll cook breakfast in the morning and we can take a ride up the intercoastal in my new boat."

Rae's eyes lit up. "I'm exhausted Stephen, do you mind if we stay?" "Of course not Rae. We can stay. Besides I've been dying to take a ride in the new boat."

I'm so happy Rae and Stephen are staying. "Wonderful, I'll go upstairs and get your room ready." "Thanks Sade, baby and I will come up with you."

Stephen gently rubbed her belly before we turned to walk away. "Sounds like a plan Javier. Rae will love that because I don't like her on the speedboat or jet skis while she's pregnant. She loves being out on the water, but I'm over protective right now."

Chapter Fourteen
Chance Encounters

Victoria

Yes! Looking fabulous in another original design by yours truly. I could stand in this full length mirror forever. Designing has been a lifesaver since losing Pierre. I've made a few new designs to add to the spring collection. This olive green, one piece, off the shoulder pant jumper is so cute and comfortable. I set it off just right with my Fendi clutch. It's one of my favorite new outfits. When I just want to relax it's perfect with a pair of flat sandals.

The entrance way to Amor Steakhouse, Las Vegas is stunning. An archway covered the walkway leading to the front doors of the restaurant. The archway was covered in an array of vibrantly colorful flowers like a mini botanical garden experience. I'm looking forward to making power moves tonight.

"Good evening. My name is Victoria, I have a reservation for two this evening." "Yes ma'am. Your guest has arrived early. He's waiting for you at the bar."

I looked toward the bar, and smiled. "I'll head to the bar. Thank you." I walked over to the bar.

Victor stood up as I got closer and extended his hand. "Funny seeing you here sir." "You look stunning this evening Victoria, it's nice seeing you again. I'm here for a business dinner meeting. Perhaps when I am done you will join me for a drink."

My smile widened. "Was that an invitation Victor?" "An invitation I hope you'll accept. You look like you could use a little spice in your night. I can show you a fun time, and get your mind off of whatever it is you came here to forget." "Invitation accepted. I am here meeting my realtor to close a business deal. Once that's done, I'll wait for you on the roof at City View Bar."

Victor looked puzzled. "Your realtor?" "Yes Victor, a commercial realtor to be exact." "I see, what's his name?" "Why the twenty questions. His name is Damion." "Wow. This world can't possibly get any smaller." Victor shook his head trying to control his laughter. Now I am confused. What is he talking about. Victor turned to stand directly in front of me. Extended his hand and began to introduce himself formerly.

"Good evening Victoria, it's a pleasure to finally meet you in person, again." Victor paused and winked at me before continuing. What did he mean by again?

"I am Victor Damion Royale, flight attendant and business owner." "Oh my goodness. I couldn't figure out why your voice seemed so familiar. This has to be the reason I felt a good vibe from you when we met on the plane. I take it Damion is the real estate guru, and Victor is the flight attendant." Following the hostess' lead, Damion escorted me to our table.

"Please bring over a bottle of your best champaign as soon as possible. We've got some celebrating to do." I leaned forward. "The gentleman is correct we have some celebrating to do, however can we switch that to a chilled bottle of your best aged bourbon." We all nodded in agreeance.

"A bourbon lover are you?" "Yes indeed Mr. Victor Damion Royale." I reached into my new Prada salmon pink briefcase and pulled out my portfolio. I placed it on the table and gathered the printed, signed contracts.

"Everything is here, in order and ready for processing. I appreciate your discretion thus far, and I hope you will continue working with me on future real estate endeavors. My lawyers have combed through all the documents. We have no further concerns. Thank you for your patience, and for working so diligently to make sure I got the venue that is best for my brand." Our drinks arrived just as I passed the portfolio across the table.

"Victoria, your brand will thrive here. I didn't expect our meeting to go this quickly. If you have no further concerns, and all documents are ready to go, I will file them first thing Monday morning." I raised my glass. "May I call you Victor from now on sir?" "Yes ma'am, you may." "Thanks Victor! I am so excited about being in Vegas and expanding my brand. Here's to new possibilities and opportunities, a night filled with Vegas sights, dancing and good vibes only." Victor's smile stretched from ear to ear. It feels marvelous to finally have my Las Vegas location locked in.

"Alright Victoria, our chariot awaits." Victor leaned over and whispered to the waitress. "Our compliments to the chef. Please share this additional tip with him." I see now, he is a generous soul. Victor tried to be as discrete as possible. However, little gets passed me. I saw him leave a one hundred dollar tip for both the chef and the waitress, yet our bill was only three hundred fifty dollars.

"Our chariot you say?" "That's right, I called a limo service for the evening. We are headed to 'O' by Cirque du Soleil at the Bellagio first."
My eyes lit up. "Marvelous, it was on my list of things to do while in Vegas." "I'm glad you approve. You'll love it Vic. Let's get moving the show starts in twenty minutes."

Two and a half hours of performance bliss. The show was breathtaking. The performers held my undivided attention. I'll definitely be seeing this with the girls when they visit. I guess I should call them soon.

"What did you think of the show?" "I thought it was phenomenal Victor. I am so glad you thought of me. I'll definitely be coming again. What's next on the agenda for the evening?" I could tell by the look in Victor's eyes that the rest of our evening was about to be spectacular. He had that you *ain't* seen nothing yet look in his eyes.

"Queen Bey has a midnight show at The Bey Hotel, the newest hotel on the strip. Doors open at midnight and the show starts at half past. By the way, The Bey Hotel is right next to the Wynn. Have I reminded you again how awesome your boutique location is?"

"Queen Bey, seriously Victor!" "Yes ma'am, close your mouth. I told you I'd be giving your mental a break this evening, and that's exactly what I intend to do Ms. Victoria."

Seating is reserved and apparently Victor knows all the right people. Our table was right in front of the stage. We had the best view in the house. As we took our seats, the waitress came to take our drink order. Victor ordered two glasses of bourbon.

Professionally Victor is a beast. Pierre and I admired that from the beginning. Personally, I'm grateful that we get along so well. I expected to be spending this trip with Pierre celebrating my latest accomplishment, and preparing for what's to come.

"Hey Vic, snap out of it. I can call you Vic, right? Where'd you go just now?" "Yes Victor, you may call me Vic. Since Pierre's passing I have my moments. I can get lost in thought without warning. I'm okay though. I just never expected to be doing this alone." "I hear you. Let's relax and watch the show. Bey is a captivating performer. You'll enjoy the show from start to finish. I guarantee it."

Victor handed me my drink. There's a sexy reassuring aura about Victor. Most importantly he makes me laugh, and I need a lot of that in my life right now. He's just easy to talk to. Easy feels good right now.

Bey's show ended at two o'clock in the morning. Victor seemed just as wired as I was. We had spent the last hour and thirty minutes singing, drinking and dancing to Queen Bey's greatest hits.

"Since you seem as wide awake as I do, let's work off our adrenaline at Ocean View. It's the best members only late night club on the strip. It brings a more grown and sexy crowd. The dress code is strictly enforced, and the DJ is the best in Vegas." "Sounds good to me Victor. I want to dance until the sun comes up. It feels good to let loose. Thanks for showing me the town tonight. This surely beats celebrating alone." "Trust me woman, I needed this evening just as much as you did. Come on, we've got some more dancing to do."

We danced until just before the sun came up. We watched the sunrise together as we walked back to my hotel. Victor saw me to the elevator, leaned in and kissed me on my cheek.

"Good night Victoria. I will call you later this afternoon to check on you. Rest well."

"You mean good morning don't you Victor?"

"Touché," Victor said bowing his head slightly.

"Thank you for everything Victor. I had a wonderful evening. It was nice to get my mind off of things and celebrate my accomplishments. I believe Pierre is smiling down on me right now. Vegas was his idea." "You're a fierce business woman Victoria. I know Pierre would be proud that you followed through. Now try to get some rest Boss Lady."

Hmmm, I kind of like how that sounds rolling off his tongue. Boss Lady, that's me.

Chapter Fifteen
Residency

Victoria

I moved into a residential suite at the Wynn Hotel to be closer to the boutique. Three months in Vegas and I'm beginning to love it here. I have only seen Victor once since our night out on the town. We've both been extremely swamped with work. We met for coffee to discuss the possibilities of me purchasing a home in Vegas. He's been sending me fabulous listings. I'll have him show us my top picks when Sade, Rae and Cher come to visit for the grand opening.

Eventually, after a couple weeks of avoiding her calls, I reached out to Sade. She listened as I poured out my heart. I needed her to understand my head space. Being the best big sister in the world, she reminded me that she is only a phone call and flight away. She promised to fill mom and the girls in. Her words echo in my thoughts. *"I am my sister's keeper, I got you always Vic."* She understood. I'm not running or hiding; I am living my life transparently understanding that it could all end in the blink of an eye. Pierre is gone, but his strength found respite within my soul. Still, I rise.

I've worked tirelessly with my publicist and brand management team to ensure the rebranding of my fashion house sets sales on fire. Focusing my energy on getting ready for the grand opening of my third location is my top priority. The ribbon cutting ceremony and grand opening is in one week. The girls will be arriving in two days. I can't wait to see everyone. Although I am enjoying making Vegas home, I miss my crew.

"Good morning Victoria, it's Miguel at the front desk. A package was delivered here for you. Would you like for someone to bring it to your room." "Thank you Miguel. Don't worry about it, I will pick it up on my way out anyway."

The package is from my soon to be brother-in-law. I wonder what's in the box. Javier is such a sentimental sweetheart. With me so far away from home, it's comforting knowing how deeply he loves Sade and the twins. Leo and Lea are blessed to have him as a stepfather. I can't wait for the wedding. I'm hoping to convince Sade to have the wedding here in Vegas. I just came up with that bright idea the other day. Destination weddings are the best.

I'm starving this morning. I need some Marco's in my life. Marco's coffee house is the best around. I stop in almost every morning after my work out for breakfast.

"Good morning Teresa. Today I'll have the avocado toast with egg whites and a caramel espresso. Make that a double shot please." "Coming right up Victoria."

My favorite seat nestled in the corner against the window offering a great strip view is available. Some mornings I sit in this seat for hours working on my book, and jotting down creative business and marketing ideas. It's hilarious. The book no one knows I'm writing. Oh well, no time to dwell on that.

"Good morning brilliant lady. How are you feeling today?" "I'm well thank you. How are you Ann?" "Business is great darling, I can't complain." "That's always good to hear. Love you mama. I'm going to head out right after I eat this morning. I have a lot still left to do in preparation for the grand opening." "I will see you there. And please Victoria, let me know if you need anything from me. I'm looking forward to meeting your sister and the girls." "Thanks Ann, I will." We air kissed and I headed out.

Ann is the owner of Marco's. She looks to be slightly older than me. We're about the same height. Her fire truck red hair greets you with flavor, and her emerald green eyes see everything. She has a loving, sarcastic demeanor that is always

144

destined to lighten the mood in any room. Sophisticated and graceful yet fierce and untamed. She's a spitfire indeed. Ann has shown me more than a few great nights out. Our friendship has been a welcomed distraction in what little down time I have.

I invited Ann to Miami when I return for Rae's baby shower in the winter. I'm still waiting to confirm the exact date before I make our reservations. We are going to stop in New York first for a few days. We'll be staying in her Manhattan loft. Most important on the list of things to do is visit Marco's of Manhattan. It's Ann's first location. There's always a special, unique love for your first location once you expand and begin to see your brand grow. I see offices in Italy, France and Switzerland in my future.

This must be my lucky day. I wonder who this brunette bombshell is that Victor has his fingers interlocked with. He is feeling himself today. There's an extra dose of confidence coated with a slight bit of arrogance in his step.

"Good morning beautiful people. I'm Victoria, it's nice to meet you." "Good morning. I'm Janelle." I leaned over and hugged Victor. "Where are you two headed this morning?"

"Hello madam Victoria, I was trying to catch you before you left Marco's. We've both been so busy lately, I thought I would surprise you." "What are you up to sir." Victor must have noticed the awkward feeling I was trying to keep from showing all over my face as I glanced at Janelle.

"Oh, and for the record, Janelle and I are just colleagues. We collaborate on a lot of business deals together. That show on the strip with us holding hands was for her ex-husband. He's been following her. We spotted him this morning right after our meeting, so we figured why not give him something to see."

"Feeling a little devious are you?" Janelle asked, smiling at Victor. "Hey sis, I'm here for you. You know I don't give a shit about dude." Yes, Victor, that I know. I appreciate you for playing along with me." "You're welcome Janelle."

"Same sob story different day Victoria. My man didn't appreciate me in any way that mattered. He became a completely different human being after we got married. I finally got fed up, and realized that I was done dealing with the blatant disrespect. I left."

"No explanation needed girlfriend. Good for you Janelle!" "I'm just running my mouth about that jackass, knowing what you've been through." Victor must have told her about Pierre's death.

"I'm doing well, no need to apologize to me. I live with my husband's memory every moment of every day. He is a part of everything I do. Even the outlandish and girly things. He's there in spirit reminding me to keep living and making myself happy."

I glanced at the time on my phone. "What did you need to see me about Victor? Was it concerning the grand opening?" "No, actually I found another home that I think trumps your favorite so far. I wanted to see your face in person when I shared the pictures. Sitting on five acres of land, it's absolutely fabulous Vic."

"Okay. I have a meeting in an hour. I'm headed back to the hotel. We can sit in the lounge for a minute before I go upstairs to prepare." Excitement filled Victor's eyes. It was as if he was getting his dream home, not finding one for a client. Looking at the gorgeous photos, I'm in love. Victor was right. This latest house has moved to the top of the list. I'm not sure I will want to see the others after visiting this one.

"When can we have a private viewing of the home? I'd like to see the property as soon as possible." Janelle surprised me, clearing her throat. "I own the property. I just let Victor know it was for sale last night. That's why we wanted to see you first thing this morning. I agreed to keep it off the market until you received first look and opportunity to buy." "Thank you both so much. I'm free this evening. Text me the address, and I will meet both of you at the house. Is six o'clock good." "It's perfect Victoria. Janelle and I will see you then. Afterwards we can go out for drinks, my treat." Janelle and I replied in unison. "You're on Victor."

Today I will wrap up all final lose ends with the event planner and project manager I hired to ensure this grand opening is well attended and goes off without a hitch. We all walked into the hotel lobby at the same time.

"Good day ladies, I reserved the conference room on the sixth floor overlooking the pool. Lunch has been prepared. Head on up and have a bite. I need to run into the business gift shop and purchase a new computer charger. I'll be up shortly."

The vibration of my cell phone startled me. I must have switched my ringer off accidentally. It's so annoying. I constantly do that.

"Hello." "Hey Vic, it's Cher." "Hey sis, whose number is this. Your name didn't pop up. I almost didn't answer." "It's a new phone. Yes, I know your ass. You'd rather wait for the voice message than run the risk of answering the phone for someone you don't want to talk to." "Damn right Cher, you already know." We both laughed. Much needed medicine on both our parts. I miss my girls a lot.

"Honey, I'm just not afraid to admit it. Everyone else does the same shit. So what's up Cher? Are you ready to come to Vegas? I can't wait to see you." "Yes Vic, that's why I'm calling. I was hoping I could come a littler earlier than everyone else. I know you have a lot going on. I won't get in the way. I just need to have a little one on one time with my Victoria."

"I know I have been distant. Grieving for me has been a journey and will continue to be. That doesn't mean I am not here for you if you need me. I just needed space to figure out how to move forward on my own. I love you Cher. You can come and stay as long as you need to. No questions asked sis. I'm here."

"My assistant is chartering me a flight now. I should get in around nine o'clock tonight. Stephen is going to fly the girls in a couple days before the opening." "Great Cher. I will leave a key for you at the front desk. I'll be out already. Make yourself at home. Freshen up, slip on a cute dress, killer heels and meet us for drinks. I'll leave the address to Ocean View on the nightstand next to my bed." "Marvelous, I'll see you tonight Vic."

I don't have time to pry right now. I have to get to my meeting. I will get all up in her head when I see her pretty face tonight. By then I will know if I want Janelle's house, and I will be celebrating finalizing the details for my grand opening.

I noticed Matthew shut down his social media pages. I wonder if there's something going on between the two of them. I've been so out of the loop lately. Oh well, tonight it is.

I waltzed in the conference room with my hair wrapped in a ball and my glasses placed on the tip of my nose. We all laughed. The ladies say I look like a professor when I host our meetings. "Alright queens, let's get down to business."

Chapter Sixteen

Celebrations & Cancelations

Victoria

Excitement filled my body as I approached Janelle's mini mansion sitting on five perfectly manicured acres. I pulled into the driveway and parked next to Victor's car. It's six o'clock. Since Victor is already here, I assume Janelle is home and ready for me. As I approached the door, I heard Janelle's voice through the intercom. "Come in Victoria the door is open."

"Oh my goodness woman, I am in love with this place already. I can't wait for my tour. Why are you selling?" "I bought another home less than a couple miles away. I was ready for a change. I lived here for five years with my ex-husband. We divorced a year ago, and I needed to start over in a new space without his memories lingering around every corner." "Enough said Janell, I understand."

I truly did understand. Although under different circumstances, I can identify with the need to start anew.

"Let's get this tour underway, Victor is in the backyard sitting by the pool waiting for us to finish." "I'm right behind you, lead the way."

Forty-five minutes later I was sold. There's six bedrooms, eight bathrooms, a gym, home office, theater and a fabulous mother-in-law suite next door to the pool house. It's perfect for my family. Plenty of room for Sade, the twins, mom and my girls.

"No negotiations needed. I accept the offer, and I'm ready to move forward." Janelle didn't hesitate. "It's yours Victoria."

Victor walked up with that *I was right gleam in his eyes.* "I knew you'd love it. The closing can be expedited. I'll get all the paperwork together, and we can finalize the details first thing in the morning." "That's awesome Victor thank you."

"I can have the keys delivered to your suite by Sunday evening." "Wow so soon Janelle, that's great." "No problem, I've already moved into my new home. I will have the remaining of my belongings cleared out by the end of the weekend."

This couldn't be more perfect. "I'm ready to celebrate." "Me too Victoria! Ladies let's get out of here. We have dinner reservations at Shi in thirty minutes."

Victor's choice in dining options did not disappoint. I didn't comment on it, but I liked the way he took the initiative to order for me. Remembering previous conversations, he chose wisely. The food was exquisite. Seared Ahi Tuna Steak and flash fried asparagus are two of my favorite dishes. The tuna was topped with a delicious garlic basil cream sauce.

The energy at the club is fierce. Janelle, Victor and I were a few shades to the wind by the time I noticed Cher making her way through the crowd. Finally, another one of my partners in crime has arrived to help me forget the hurt.

"Hey sis, over here." I waved my hand as she looked up to scope out the VIP sections. Our eyes met. Cher looked so relieved to have spotted me. The table was stocked with bottles. I poured a glass of Jack Honey and handed it to her as soon as she made her way to our section.

"Cheers! I finally made it. Thanks love, Jack Honey, you know what I need." "Yes Cher, I heard it in your voice when we talked. It's so good to see you. You're looking sexy as always. I see you showing off those washboard abs. I'm loving this mini skirt and halter young lady. You're definitely making a statement queen Cher."

"I hope the statement is clear!" "Oh yes Cher, it's crystal clear." "Tonight I'm just happy to be almost three thousand miles from home. I've missed you Vic." "No worries Cher, we're about to party and let loose. There's plenty of time to catch up on reality tomorrow. I got you woman." "Thanks Vic."

I don't think I've seen Cher dance this hard in years. Ann hit it off with Cher and Janelle instantly.

"Another shot of whiskey ladies? This round is on me." Before anyone could respond to Janelle, Cher spoke up. For whatever reason, tonight was long overdue for her. "Thanks Janelle, make mine a double."

Cher winked at Janelle and pulled me back to the center of the dance floor. She had one of my arms, while I used the other to pull Ann in with me. When we returned Victor was waiting for us. He motioned for me to come closer and dance with him. Suddenly a stroke of bashfulness washed over me. He could sense the hesitation in my approach. He softened his smile and reached for my hand. Before I could react, his arms were wrapped around my waist.

"It's my turn now. I've watched you avoid me all night. Don't forget dear Victoria, one of my greatest attributes is patience." "Victor, I have a feeling you won't let me forget." "You're absolutely right woman."

There's a subtle chemistry between the two of us that frightens me to the core. Victor's support has been monumental since I have been in Vegas. He's been a behind the scenes integral part of my success here. His friendship is important to me, and that's all I can handle right now. I appreciate his patience.

Victor called a limo for Janelle and Ann. We weren't far from my suite, so we walked from Ocean View. The sky was full of stars. I glanced over at Victor and caught him looking up at the sky as if he was trying to make out the constellations.

Cher is three steps ahead of us skipping to her own beat. At least she had tonight to let loose. I am dying to know what the hell is going on with Cher and Matthew.

"Beautifully peaceful, isn't it?" "Yes Victor, after all I've been through, I still hold hope for my future." "Hope gives you the strength to continue rising. Good night ladies." Victor spoke with such confidence. He pressed the elevator button for us.

"Congratulations on your new home again. I'm happy you'll be staying for a while." "Thanks Victor, this evening was just what the doctor ordered." That was so corny. Did I really just throw the same line he used right back at him.

"Thank you for taking care of us tonight. It was nice to meet you Victor." Cher gave him a hug and disappeared into the elevator.

"Good night Sir Victor." "Good night Queen Victoria."

As soon as the doors shut Cher started laughing. "Queen Victoria, Sir Victor seems to have a little crush on the queen. Did I read that wrong?" "I don't know Cher, we are just business associates. That's all I can offer at the moment." "Well sis, let me enlighten you. Sir Victor is definitely interested in far more than a professional relationship, and he doesn't seem concerned with how long he may have to wait to get what he wants."

Cher is so right about Victor being a patient man. Waiting on me, he'll prove to be the most patient man I've ever met. Right now all this soul can manage is taking care of self, and giving one thousand percent to all of my business and investment endeavors.

"I hear you Cher. We need to get some sleep. We have a mountain of catching up to do tomorrow missy. I left you alone tonight, but tomorrow you're mine." "Yes Queen Mother Victoria." "Girl stop. Goodnight Cher. Get some rest. Mentally, we are both going to need it." "Goodnight Vic." I turned on my calm ocean sounds and drifted off to sleep.

My senses were awakened by the sweet smells of home. I can smell my mama's homemade blueberry pancakes, bacon, roasted potatoes and coffee filling the air. It's good to have Cher all to myself for a few days.

"Good morning sweetness, it smells like home in here." "Good morning Vic. I figured it's the least I can do for my gracious hostess." "Your hostess appreciates it. I've missed your cooking Cher." I pulled out a bottle of Single Barrel Select and added a shot to our coffee cups. "Cheers Cher. I'm glad you're here." We both sipped slowly.

"Now, what the fuck is going on. Why are you really here?" "I'm here to support you Victoria. You are opening your third location you know." "Don't bullshit me Cher, you know what I mean. Why are you here early? What are you running, or shall I say hiding from?" "I'm not fucking hiding, I'm dying slowly inside, and I didn't want anyone to know what was happening to me. I spent so much time focused on my career, that I couldn't see what was happening right under my nose."

"Under your nose? What the hell Cher." "Matthew has been cheating on me, and I haven't told a soul. Well, he knows I know now."

"Matthew! Not our man of the year. What!" Cher rolled her eyes at me. "He's not the saint we all thought he was. I'm not sure when it started. I was so preoccupied with work and silently suffering from our miscarriage. The miscarriage happened before we could even tell anyone we were expecting."

"Shit Cher. You had a miscarriage?" Wiping the tears streaming down Cher's face, I'm in shock. She nodded.

"Then, when Rae and Stephen announced their pregnancy to everyone, it felt like casting a shadow to bring it up." "I wish you hadn't felt the need to go through that without the support of your girls. We love you Cher." "I know you do Vic."

I downed my spiked coffee, picked up the Single Barrel bottle and took it to the head.

"So how the fuck does this lead to Matthew cheating on you?" "It doesn't." "I'm lost Cher." I chugged another mouth full.

"I really don't know for sure how long he was cheating. I thought he was always working or with me, but I was wrong. I think the more wrapped up I became in the success of my businesses, the less time we had to spend together."

"You always seem perfectly fine when we are able to get together." "I know Vic, but it's an act. We weren't arguing or anything obnoxious. I think

159

we just drifted apart. Somehow, as usual, my good just wasn't good enough."

Cher stood up abruptly. She ran to the restroom and let loose. "I've been nauseous most of the day, every day, since I saw him in bed with another woman." "What? Where Cher?" "It happened a couple of days before the bombing. I guess no one noticed how unconcerned I was about my precious Bourbon Princess blowing to pieces."

"I don't think any of us thought about it Cher. All I could focus on was Pierre being murdered. I still have vivid nightmares. I wish you had told one of us." "I know sis, but I couldn't. For a while I wasn't sure who I could trust." "What the hell Cher. So now you're questioning our loyalty. Rae and Sade have always had your back, and you know I do too."

"We know her Vic." "So who the fuck is it Cher?" Cher looked away. "Shit Cher. Spill it." "Grace!" Cher screamed her name from the depths of her soul. "No way! Sade's nanny and new business partner is who you think Matthew is having an affair with. Really Cher?" "I don't damn think Vic, I know. Do you think Sade knew?" "Now you're grasping at straws Cher. There's no way my sister knew this was happening and said nothing."

"I picked up on awkward vibes from Grace at Javier at Sade's party. We had never spent much time together. Although I've hung out around she and Sade, I don't know her on a personal level. I figured she got Matthew's contact information from Sade, because she started taking shooting lessons from Matthew."

"Matthew and Grace? Shit, I can't imagine Matthew with anyone but you." "Well, think about how I felt. I finally trusted in a man again. I let my walls come crumbling down. Why?" "Beating yourself up isn't the answer Cher. You have to tell Sade. She would never have kept Grace in her life if she knew this side of her."

"I did my own research Victoria. I discovered that Grace wasn't just the nanny and a trusted friend to the university president's family." "You mean the family she worked for prior to working for Sade." "Yes, Vic that's exactly what I mean. His wife discovered they were having an affair. Shortly thereafter, she found out Grace was pregnant. In order to save his marriage, Grace was forced to relinquish full custody to the father and guardianship to his wife."

"This is unbelievable Cher. They must have worked hard to keep this scandal under wraps. So you're telling me that Grace is the biological mother of their youngest child. Wow!"

My head feels like it's on a turntable being scratched repeatedly. I just knew Cher and Matthew were solid. This is why I don't think I can ever trust my heart to fall in love again.

"Exactly Vic. They have friends in high places. Legally, Grace can never speak of the child or the family. She is not permitted to initiate communication."

"Cher, how did you get all this information?" "How I got the information is not important. What is important is Sade knowing she was a target." "What do you mean Cher?" "Okay Vic, think about it. If we believe that Sade had no idea what Grace was up to then we must assume that Sade was a mark. Grace targeted her. She was out of a job and needed a new home to prepare for her next scheme."

"My sweet Sade was vulnerable after the Joshua-Antonio fiasco. I guess she didn't look into Grace's past as thoroughly as she should have." "No, she didn't Vic."

"I'm so sorry Cher. Sade is going to hold herself responsible. That I am sure of. Damnit." "After wiggling her way into Sade's heart, she focused her desires on my man. I was so dumb and naïve, I actually believed he would never hurt me in any way." "Back up Cher. How did you catch him in the act? And for the record, we all were snowed by Grace. I never would have suspected she'd do something like this. We all knew her through Sade. I liked her until now. I can't believe this madness." "Hmm, you can't believe it Vic. Again, how do you think I feel?" "I don't know Cher, but you better never get it in your head that you can't reach out to us for help! You did the same shit with Sebastian. You're always there for us no matter what. You have to be open to receiving the same." "I know Vic. I know."

"Let's circle back to my original question. Cher, how did you catch him in the act?" "Matthew was in the shower after our morning workout together. I came down to the kitchen to get a couple bottles of water. Our home phone rang. I answered, but no one said anything. That happened three times consecutively."
That's childish. "Three times, really. That seems suspicious, who does that. I'm sorry Cher, continue." I could only offer a blank stare. My blood is boiling.

"I went upstairs and stepped into the shower. I began to wash Matthews back and he asked me who was on the phone. I told him I didn't know and that whomever it was called three times and said nothing each time." "How did he react to that." "His reaction is what made me suspicious." "So what did he do Cher?" "He turned to me, rinsed off abruptly and said he had to meet a client. It was just after seven o'clock in the morning. As long as we have been together, he has never had to meet a client that early in the morning."

"Did you ask where he was going?" "No Vic. I just watched him walk away. I was thinking that there was something major going on with one of his high profile clients. I am accustomed to not prying about his work, because I know he can't share. I knew that when we got together. As a private contractor, his special operation assignments are constant. That morning just felt different."

Cher paused and stared at me. I know she sees the anger flooding my eyes. I could shoot that asshole on sight. I'm trying to process what Cher is telling me. My heart is breaking for her. "Damnit Vic why me?" "Why any of us Cher? Please continue." I grabbed Cher's hands to try and steady them.

"When I walked out of the restroom, I heard him in the study talking low. I could only catch the tail end of the conversation." "Okay, what did you catch?"

"Meet me at the dock at ten tonight. She will be gone. I will be alone. Then he hung up."

"Meet him at the dock. What dock?" "I assume he meant mine. He knew I was going to be on the island, and I didn't take the Bourbon Princess. I was going with my assistant Christina. Sometimes we ride over on her boat. Anyway, I was overly suspicious by that point. I wanted to know what was going on." "I don't blame you sis."

"I decided to let Christina go without me to take care of business. I stayed away from the house until just before ten that night. A dodge pulled up with pitch black tinted windows. I knew I had seen that car before, but in the moment I couldn't put my finger on it."

I remembered that Grace has a car like that. "Grace recently purchased a car matching that description." "Correct Vic, but like I said, in the moment I couldn't recall why the vehicle looked familiar." "I hear you Cher. I don't know what would have been going through my mind in that moment."

Sade and Rae are going to lose it when they find out. I wonder if the men knew about this.

Cher's mouth continued to move as my wheels began to turn faster. "Matthew walked up to the driver side door and opened it. He held out his hand as if to assist the person getting out. She elegantly stood up. Matthew shut the door behind her, and lead her into my home. He was wearing a blue suit that I picked out by the way. She was wearing a blue contoured dress that hugged her flawless physique in all the right places. Instantly I knew it was a date, and not a meeting with a client."

"You mean you saw her from the moment she got out of the car and you just hid. Cher, I don't know if I could have done that." "You know I'm calculated, I had to take it all in. Besides, I hadn't caught them doing anything but walking into the house. I watched them greet each other far more passionately once inside. He kissed her for what seemed like an hour."

"And your ass still didn't barge in. Cher, everyone in sight would have been dead on sight!" "Nope Vic, I didn't. I turned the security cameras back on. I assume he switched them off so I couldn't find out. I watched from the cameras in the office. He had no idea I was home. He treated her to a candlelight dinner, and topped it off with a glass of my special reserved twenty-five year aged bourbon. He gave that bitch bourbon from my do not disturb stash."

How dare he bring another bitch, I don't care who she is, to the home he shares with his fiancé. That's outright disgusting.

"Cher, how did you not rush out and beat the shit out of both of them. He better be glad you didn't have one of his many guns in hand." Cher grunted slightly. "Well, actually I did. After I saw that my mood shifted from shock to anger real quick." My frown curled upward slightly. "It's about damn time Cher."

"Oh it gets better Vic. He took her aboard the Bourbon Princess. By the time I switched the cameras on in the yacht, she was standing naked before him. He picked her up and fucked her everyway from Sunday. I plugged into the security app on my phone, and took a long dreaded walk to my yacht. I didn't miss a stroke. I walked in quietly. The sounds of their moaning drowned my thinking."

> "I need all of you. Please don't make me wait this long again Matthew." "It's yours baby, take it."

"His response to her desire for him echoed in my mind repeatedly. I cocked the gun and aimed it at the back of her head. Matthew heard the sound lifted her up off of him, and lunged toward me. She disappeared without saying a word. I was left in the bed of their sins with him. I ran back to the house, and locked myself in our room for the rest of the night. I cried until the sun came up."

"How have you been coping?" "He blew up our relationship. As much as I love him, I will never trust him again. I just buried it, and we both focused on you. When the shit hit the fan nothing else mattered. Your safety trumped my heartbreak. You know me Vic."

"Yes, I know you Cher. I can't stand that about you, because you won't allow others to reciprocate the same behavior. You don't have to hold the weight of the world on your shoulders every second of your life Cher. Can Christina run things on the east coast for a while?" "Yes Vic, Christina can run the entire business without me. She's a remarkable business woman, and I trust her."

"Perfect! I think you need to stay with me and clear your mind in peace. You need to design your plan for moving forward. I love you Cher, please say you'll stay in Vegas with me for a while."

"Thank you, yes I will stay. I can't go back there. I don't know if the guys know anything. I'm so embarrassed. We agreed to keep it quiet until he was completely moved out of my home. He's claiming to love only me, but my walls a all the way up. He broke my trust in him. I don't know why, but it hurts worse than my break up with Sebastian. I know no one is perfect Vic, but I didn't see this coming. Cheating on me was the last thing I ever expected Matthew to do."

My heart is breaking for Cher. "I miss Pierre like fucking hell. I would bet my life that he had no idea Matthew was having an affair with Grace. He would have forced Matthew to tell you the truth. It's just how he is. I think Javier and Stephen would do the same."

"Vic, the fact that your husband had just been killed made me feel selfish to even consider burdening you with my issues. We all knew you needed to grieve in your own way. I certainly didn't want to pounce this bullshit in your lap. It all happened back to back. I just swallowed it whole, and played the role of the happy, newly engaged fiancé."

"Okay Cher, I am here now. You're not going through this alone. We have spent most of the day talking about the pain. Time to give it a rest. Go shower and change. We are going to lunch then shopping for your new Vegas wardrobe. You'll be with me for a while." "I don't want to tell the girls until after your grand opening. I just want the energy focused on you and your accomplishments. That's why they are coming. We can fill them in on the gory details of my ex-fiancé after we celebrate our Queen Victoria."

As always, Cher is putting someone else's needs first. "My mouth is sealed. No worries Cher, and thank you for always being supportive no matter what turmoil you're going through." "Always Vic, I am my sister's keeper."

Our love runs deep, and there is nothing we wouldn't do for each other. I just hate to my core that Cher felt she had to suffer, yet again, in silence. I thought I got through to her after I found out what she was enduring with Sebastian years ago.

Chapter Seventeen

Early Arrivals

Victoria

I get to move into the house today. I haven't told anyone about the house. Cher will find out after breakfast. I can't wait to see the look on her face. I wasted no time. I have all of my furniture being delivered tomorrow.

"Good morning sunshine. I didn't realize you were awake. We have breakfast reservations this morning. Wheels up in forty." "Morning Vic, I'm famished. I'll be ready in thirty."

"Cool, I made you some tea. It's on the counter. I'm hopping in the shower."

My phone started buzzing and cut off my music. I guess I forgot to turn my ringer back on from last night. I didn't want to be disturbed once my head finally hit the pillow. "Hello." "Hey Vic it's Stephen. I'm not sure what's going on, but Rae is making me bring her and Sade to Vegas tonight. I just thought I'd warn you. They won't tell me why they are coming earlier than expected. What the hell is going on."

"I don't know Stephen. Send me the itinerary. It's okay I miss them both. I'll take excellent care of Rae. You know I got you." Stephen forwarded the flight information to me.

"Let's get out of here Cher. Our day just got more interesting." "Right behind you Vic."

Breakfast was amazing as usual. I love Hazel's diner. I must eat Mr. Barnes French toast special at least once a week. I love this quaint whole in the wall café.

"Hazel, please tell Mr. Barnes thank you. I appreciate all the extra love he put into my French toast this morning." "Yes ma'am, I sure will. It was nice to meet you Cher, I hope you'll dine with us again while you're in town." "Hazel you know as long as she's with me, she will be back." "See you in a few days Vic."

I waved at Hazel once more as we headed out. I need to stop at the house first to make sure everything has been removed. I also need to make sure the cleaning service did a good job.

"Where are we headed next Vic." "It's a surprise. I promise you'll love it."

We pulled into my new driveway. I jumped out of the car before Cher could ask where we were. I started for the front door. Cher got out and followed me. I unlocked the door, and Cher gave me the most puzzled look.

"Welcome to my new home." I turned to see the look on Cher's face as the words were leaving my mouth.

"I love it. I need a tour now. Wait, when did you decide to stay in Vegas? I thought it was just temporary. I never imagined you'd stay long enough to need a home." "I don't need one Cher, I want one. I like it here, and I needed a clean break from everything that reminds me of Pierre. I can't move on in Miami. Maybe someday I will move back permanently, but for now I consider myself bicoastal."

"I support your decision Vic. I understand. I appreciate the offer to let me stay." "Always and forever, I got your back. I know this is going to be a heart-wrenching process Cher, but eventually you will begin to heal. Healing will manifest one day at a time sis. Thank the Lord you had not gotten married yet. Knowing you, he wouldn't have been asked to sign a prenuptial agreement."

"Enough, I am ready for a tour. No more Matthew talk. So tell me Vic, how the hell did you fall into this little piece of paradise?"

"It literally fell into my lap less than a week ago." "This is a nice gem to have fall into your lap." "Tell me about it Cher. It was brought to me at the right time, and I couldn't pass it up. I am putting our Ft. Lauderdale Condo and the Coral Gables home on the market. I will take part of the profit and invest it in a stunning ocean view three bedroom condo in Bal Harbor."

"Seems to me that you've got it all planned out Vic. If you're happy, I'm happy for you sis." "Thank you Cher. I just keep putting one foot in front of the other. Some nights I cry myself to sleep and other nights I sit up laughing at old photos. My goal is to keep getting up in the morning and making the best of the new day." "I'm honored that I get to be your first house guest Vic." "I'm glad you're here too Cher."

I threw my arms around her neck and just held her for a minute. Quietly, I think we both needed it.

"Now we have to run to the store to pick up a bottle of bubbly and a few air mattresses. The next surprise is that Javier called to give me a heads up. Rae and Sade asked him to bring them to Vegas tonight. He said Rae was adamant but wouldn't say why. My guess is somehow Sade found out about Grace and told Rae when she couldn't find you." "You're probably right Vic. I wasn't going to call Sade or Rae to tell them I was here until the morning of our flight."

"Pandora's box is wide open now Cher. Rae and Sade fly in tonight."

Cher's cheeks were flushed. Talking about whatever the hell went down with all of us isn't going to be easy. It's rare that she lets anyone catch her in such a vulnerable state. Through the years she's learned to build a fortress around her heart.

"Honey tonight is tonight. Snap out of it. I already know what went down. No need to clam up on me now. We will deal with later, later." Exhaling together, we headed for the door.

What is he doing here. A pop up? "Welcome home Victoria. I had to stop by and bring you a housewarming gift. I know, unannounced, but I was in the neighborhood." "Give me a hug fool. Thanks Victor." "You're welcome. When's the furniture coming?" "All of my furniture arrives early tomorrow morning. We were actually headed to the store now." "Oh okay. I'll let you ladies get to it. Call me in the morning when the movers get here. If you need me, I'll stop by to help?" "Thanks Victor, you know I will hold you to it." "Yes ma'am, I know you will."

"I've decided we're staying here tonight since everyone will be in town. I was going to move us from the hotel suite tomorrow anyway. We just need to run and pick up a few essentials to make it through the night. My sister and other best friend

are flying in early. They arrive later tonight."
"Gotcha. Don't forget to call me in the morning if you need my help." "Thanks a million Victor."
"The satisfied look on your face right now is all the appreciation I need."

Victor's smile had a way of calming the roughest of seas surging inside of me. He definitely found me a jewel. I love my new home. I waved goodbye once more before closing the door. His walk exuded such confidence, and his actions felt genuine.

"Vic, you deserve all the happiness you're feeling right now. Pierre would be proud of you."
"I really believe he would be proud of me Cher. He always pushed me beyond my furthest point."

"As a true partner should Vic. Maybe Sade and Rae can focus on all your good news and energy instead of worrying about me." "Don't count on it Cher. I know Sade is on fire if she knows about Grace. Come on sis, put your seatbelt on. We'll pick up what we need, grab some take out and come back to the house to chill. I arranged for a car to pick them up from the airport and bring them here."

"I'm so keeping these shades." "Correction Cher, you are wearing my shades that you will put right back where you picked them up from." "Then we need to stop and pick me up a pair of my own. Comfort shopping is a welcomed activity right about now. Chanel shades here I come."

"Girl you're mess, and I know you're serious." "As a heart attack Vic. What's up with Stephen and Javier? Are they staying or turning around?"

"They were turning around originally, but he and Javier were able to work out their schedules. They are going to stay at The Belmont. The Belmont is home to the hottest new casino on the strip. They both have been dying to christen the poker tables."

I know how demanding Rae can be on any given day. With pregnancy, she's kicked it up a thousand notches. Stephen is a trooper though. He is able to bring her down to size quite gently when necessary.

"I'm nervous about my surprise for Rae. Stephen has been an angel helping me maneuver behind the scenes." "What surprise Vic?" "Rae's cosmetics will have shelf life in all of my boutiques. We will reveal her line as our signature line of beauty to compliment House of V designs."

It's nice to see excitement instead of worry in Cher's eyes. "Honey Rae's excitement might cause her to go into early labor. What an amazing opportunity."

"We have a lot to celebrate, and we also will be right beside you in the muck pulling your ass out. You're not alone Cher. Fuck Matthew. Sure, I loved and believed in him wholeheartedly too. At the end of the day sis, he is a man. Period. He is not perfect. He made a choice. Now he must rest in the consequences of his choice."

"I love you Vic." "I love you too sis. We got you."

"I wonder if Javier and Stephen know." "I doubt it Cher. Stephen didn't know why Rae insisted on arriving early. He just knew if he didn't bring her, she'd get here on her own. There's no way in hell he was having that. Don't be surprised if it comes out on the plane ride here though. I am sure Javier and Stephen will be asking questions."

"I guess we wait and see. It's not like I did anything wrong. It's just so humiliating to talk about." "I know the pain of secrets and self-prescribed humiliation. Stop stressing over what you think people will think of you. He did this to the two of you."

I pulled into one of the takeout parking spaces. The Lucky Lobster parking lot is packed as usual. Customers are wrapped around the building waiting in line for tables. The food is definitely worth the wait, but I am not in the mood today. I'm so glad we ordered takeout.

"I'm going in to pick up our order. Pull yourself together Cher. We are going home to relax, and not blame ourselves for the weight of the world."

"I'm with you Vic."

Our ride home was quiet. I was deep in thought running through my grand opening speech for House of V, and wondering how to keep Cher's mind off of Matthew. Time flies when I wish it would creep, and it creeps when I wish it would fly. Rae and Sade will be here in just over an hour. It's after eight already. This has been a long eventful day. I officially set up shop in Vegas. I'm not yet sure how much grass I'll let grow under my feet here before I surprise us all with the next adventure. What I do know, is that life is too short to limit myself.

"This seafood smells delicious. Come on Cher, here's your apron. It's time to grub." "You don't have to tell me twice. There's nothing like scrumptious cuisine that I didn't have to make!" "I heard that Cher, but you know you'll always be our favorite chef!"

"Turn the music up Vic. I need to drown out all the conversations in my head. We will be good and toasty by the time Rae and Sade arrive."

I popped open a bottle of my moonshine and poured us a sip.

"Cheers to new beginnings Cher." "Yes please, cheers to new beginnings Vic."

Chapter Eighteen

House of V

Victoria

What a beautiful sunrise this morning. I have finished my first morning swim in my new home. I feel rejuvenated. The movers will be here shortly. I turned the intercom on so my voice could echo through the house.

"Good morning my beautiful sisters. Breakfast is ready. Coffee has been brewed and the movers arrive in thirty minutes."

One by one I hear the pitter patter of brilliant souls coming towards the kitchen. My heart is full having us all together again. I've missed the girls even though I needed the time apart. We all heal differently. I'm not sure I'll ever fully get over losing Pierre. I just hope each day I continue to get stronger. I know he'd want that for me.

I pulled Sade and Rae aside last night before they could go in on Cher. I let them know that it wasn't a good time to dig. Cher wants to focus only on my grand opening right now, and I love her for it. It was hard, especially for Sade, but they both agreed to honor my wishes.

"I plan to spend the entire day getting the house in order. I invited Javier and Stephen over for dinner tonight so they can see my new place."

"Vic, we are here to help wherever you need. Now about my man, you'll have to pry him from the poker table." "Oh he'll be here Rae. Stephen and Javier can gamble all they want after dinner. I told them to come over at six this evening."

"The movers are here ladies," Rae called out from the front door. She pulled the door open as the truck was straightening up in the driveway.

Sade's uber pulled up right after the moving truck. She's headed to have breakfast with Javier.

"Kisses sis, I love you. Tell Javier I said hi and have fun." "See you ladies when I return. I'll be back in a couple of hours, and I'll dive right in to help. I Love you too Vic."

"Now the real fun can begin. As a reminder ladies, this is your home too. I will come back to south Florida once the house and condo are sold to purchase a new place. Until then, when I visit I'll just be crashing with you guys. Just know that you're not getting rid of me, and as I stated, this is your home too. We are bicoastal now queens."

"We know you're not abandoning us Vic. We love you. We are proud of you for picking your shit up, and doing what you had to do to keep pushing forward. Besides, when Stephen gets here for dinner I'll be telling him I want to stay for another week or two. I need a little break from Miami."

I know Stephen won't mind. Rae totally made my day with that news. He loves Vegas he'll either stay too, or just fly back to pick Rae up when she's ready to go back to Miami. This just makes my news so much more exciting. I can't wait to tell her that we want to carry her line of cosmetics in our stores.

"Rae, you may stay as long as you like. You can help me finish all the decorating details over the next couple weeks. It will be perfect. Cher is staying for a bit too, I couldn't be happier."

"Yes, chef Cher will be here with you ladies. Now we need to get to work. Vic, you and Rae stay downstairs and direct the movers. Since our talk earlier, I know where everything goes upstairs. I will stay upstairs to help."

"Good morning, you must be Victoria, I recognize your voice from our conversation." "Yes sir you are correct. Good morning."

"Great, my name is Zaire, the delivery on sight crew manager." "It's nice to meet you Zaire. These are my sisters, Cher and Rae. Cher will be upstairs. If the movers have questions regarding any of the rooms on the second level they may ask her."

"Yes ma'am, we'll get started right away. Based on the order, we should have all the furniture in and assembled within three hours." "That's wonderful. Thank you Zaire." "You're welcome."

"Rae, I need to run into my office and return a phone call about the grand opening. Peep in if you need me, otherwise relax and supervise."

I could hear Rae laughing as I walked into my office. She is good at relaxing and telling other people what to do. She is growing into pregnancy quite nicely.

I walked into the office and calmly shut the door behind me. My nerves are going haywire. I began to shake uncontrollably. Inhaling deeply and exhaling, I try to steady my breathing. This usually helps calm my nerves. My phone won't stop vibrating. I've been hitting ignore for the last hour. I hope the girls didn't notice. The number is showing as unknown. Whomever it is keeps leaving the same message on my voicemail. I have received five messages thus far.

> *I will keep calling until you answer. This is not a game. I see the moving truck in your driveway, I know you're home. You can run, but from me you will never hide.*

His voice sounded identical to TJ's voice. What the fuck is going on here. I thought that motherfucker blew up on the Bourbon Princess with Pierre. He has exposed my darkest hour, stalked and tortured me emotionally, murdered my husband and now this. When will it end Lord? When? I guess it won't be now.

My phone vibrated off the edge of the desk and hit the floor. Tears streaming down my face, I could feel my blood boiling. My body temperature is rising fast. Oh no, this isn't happening right now. Breathe Victoria, breathe. I picked up my phone, and stared at my newly cracked screen.

"Hello. Hello." All I can hear is breathing on the other end of the phone. Who the hell sends cryptic voicemails demanding you answer, but says nothing when you do?

"Who the fuck is this? What the hell do you want. You said answer asshole. Hello!"

I don't know how long she's been standing there, but I saw Sade in the doorway staring at me when I turned around.

"Did you really think I would watch you for years waiting patiently to finally punish you for what you did to my father, just to kill myself in a bombing. Hell no bitch, I wanted you to suffer like I did. You have lost the most important man in your life and now maybe you can feel a little of the pain I felt."

"Fuck you and your father. You're a psychotic bastard."

Sade snatched the phone from my hands and lit into TJ. "Your father raped and abused me. You are nothing more than the devil's spawn. Consider this a warning. I will kill you if you come near my sister or any of my family."

Sade ended the call. She pulled out her phone and called Javier. "Get your ass back here now babe, and bring Stephen. Hurry!" "Ok Sade we're on our way."

"Rae! Cher!" "Yes, Sade we're coming. What the hell is going on?" Rae was panting between words trying to move as fast as she could.

I glanced at the time. Shit I've been sitting in this office for over two hours. I didn't even hear Sade come back from breakfast. The movers must have finished faster than expected. Thank goodness Rae and Cher were here to help. They both came running into my office.

"Sade my ass is too big to be running around. What's wrong. Mama Rae can't move that fast these days."

Sade pointed at me. She couldn't speak, her eyes were bloodshot. She looked at Rae rolled her eyes and stormed off screaming.

"That motherfucker is not dead! I want to douse him in gasoline and watch his body burn slowly. I'll find pleasure in listening to him cry out in agony. He's all mine."

"What's going on Vic. What is Sade ranting about. Speak to us honey. Cher and I need to understand what's happening. Who is not dead?"

"TJ!" His name echoed. I screamed it as loud as I could.

"TJ?" I thought he died in the explosion. Oh hell no, is at the real phone call you had to make Vic?" Rae was looking confused, waiting for a response.

Cher squared off with me. We were so close she could have given me mouth to mouth. Her eyes started squinting, and I knew I had about five seconds to start talking before she let loose on everyone and thing in sight.

"Cher, Rae, I'm sorry. I don't know what to say really. Sade walked in on the conversation. I was trying to keep it from all of you."

"Keep what from us Vic." Rae was growing impatient. She started breathing heavy. This isn't what I wanted. I don't want her stressed while she's carrying her precious baby.

"At least sit down Rae, and I will explain." Rae sat down immediately. "Okay Vic speak."

"I started receiving phone calls from an unknown number. For about a week I ignored it, because I figured it was telemarketers. Then today, I received several calls from an unknown number, this time the person left a message. The same message was left each time. When I heard the voice on my voicemail this morning I panicked. It sounded just like TJ."

"What does the message say Vic?" Cher questioned me, but wasn't waiting for an answer. She picked up my phone and played the message aloud.

Rae glanced down at her phone. "Javier just text me. He and Steven are four minutes away."

I could hear my sister making noise upstairs but couldn't tell what the hell she was doing.

Javier and Stephen walked through the door just as Sade was coming down the stairs. Javier looked at his fiancé hugging Betty, our father's Nine millimeter.

"Babe you okay?" Javier asked as Sade made her way downstairs.

"No. Nothing is okay. Everything is all fucked up and it's my fault. Because my sister protected me, she is being punished. I can't take this shit anymore Javier. I will kill that son of a bastard my damn self. I will watch him squirm until his last breath. This time I will end it."

Javier grabbed Sade. He carefully removed her finger from the trigger, and slid the gun from her grip.

"Rae start talking," Stephen demanded knowing Sade couldn't speak yet.

"Stephen everything is fucked up. TJ didn't die in the explosion. Somehow he escaped. He has spent the time since the explosion continuing to stalk Victoria. He's been watching her every move it seems. She just discovered all of this today. She had been receiving calls from an unknown caller, and today the caller decided to leave voice messages. We listened to the messages earlier. He left the same message each time. Vic finally answered today, and Sade happened to overhear. She snatched the phone from Vic and cursed TJ out. Sade called Javier and took off upstairs. Now we know what she went to get."

"That was a mouthful Rae. Damn this man."

Cher sat next to me on the love seat. Javier got Sade to sit with him on the couch next to Rae and Stephen.

"Welcome to my new home everyone. I thought this would be my place to begin anew. Our past will haunt us forever it seems." My heart was breaking slowly all over again. The explosion keeps replaying in my mind.

"I am my sister's keeper." Cher said the words with conviction. She placed her hand out in front of her. Then she put my hand on top of hers.

"I am my sister's keeper." As the words left my lips, tears began streaming down my face. Where would I be without my sisters.

Rae and Sade spoke in unison. Sade placed her hand on top of mine and interlocked our fingers. And as always, Rae slapped her hand on top.

"Now I wish a motherfucker would try us again. Pregnant or not, my trigger finger is ready."

My heart knows Rae meant every word. I love my sisters for life.

Javier and Stephen gave each other the brotherly nod and excused themselves. We were all startled out of our silent stare by the doorbell.

"Damn. I forgot I invited Victor over to meet you guys."

"Don't worry about it Vic. Rae get the door. I will get in the kitchen and start getting dinner together. The guys will want to meet anyone you're around now. It may be a little tense tonight. However, Victor may have some local connections to law enforcement that can help us with the disastrous monster that is TJ."

"You're right. Thank you Cher." "That's what sisters are for. Rae and I can handle things downstairs for now. You and Sade go upstairs and freshen up. We need to eat and work out a plan of action. Period."

Sade and I went upstairs as Cher ordered. For the first thirty minutes we held each other and sat in silence.

"Sade I'm sorry that this keeps coming back to surface. I thought killing Theodore for raping you years ago would be the end of that nightmare. Now his son is back again with a vengeance. He just wants to make me suffer for taking his father from him. He doesn't care why I did it."

"Vic you can't apologize for saving me from Theodore. Please don't apologize. TJ is sick. We will catch his ass. Don't worry sis. Let's get downstairs so we can eat something and figure out what we do next." "Okay Sade, let's go."

"The House of V grand opening is coming up, and I wanted everything to be perfect. Now I can't even think straight." "The House of V grand opening will go off without a hitch. You have my word Vic. Now take a deep breath and come on." "I love you Sade, thank you for being the best big sister a girl could hope for." "I love you more little sis."

By the time we made our way back downstairs, Javier and Stephen were filling Victor in on the madness. I gave them permission to let Victor know what was going on. I decided after Pierre's death that I deserved not to be ashamed of my past. Victor and I were becoming good friends, and he's far more familiar with the city than we are.

"The Lasagna smells marvelous Cher." "Thank you my sweet Victoria."

Rae handed me a glass of merlot, and I finished it in one gulp. Apparently she expected me to, because she was still standing there waiting to pour me another.

"You have to drink my portion too since baby and I can't partake. I know you can handle it Auntie Vic." "I love you Rae."

Victor stood up, and gave me a hug. "Welcome to my new home. You've met my people."

"I felt like I knew them already, you've told me so much about them. I appreciate you inviting me to dinner. Javier and Stephen told me what's been happening. I won't ask questions. I am here if you want to talk to me about whatever you need. In the meantime, I called my home security company and let Stephen talk to them. They will be here in the morning to set up your new security system."

For some reason my nerves seemed to settle slightly as Victor spoke. There is a calming, reassuring presence about him.

"Thank you for your help Victor." "You're welcome Victoria. Now that I know you have concerns, I will make sure there is heightened security at the House of V grand opening. And no, you didn't ask me to do that, but I am. Now walk outside with me. A little fresh air will be good for you. Cher said dinner will be ready in a few."

Wine in hand, Victor distracted me for another twenty minutes while the others talked in circles about how to handle TJ.

"Dinner is ready family." Cher called out for us to come to the table.

"Before we start I want to give a toast. I know the gates of hell just opened up on me again, but I feel like good news will give me fuel to keep fighting." All eyes fixated on me.

"Rae, I was going to wait until the grand opening to share this news with you." "Share what Vic?" Rae had a sense of uncertainty in her voice.

"House of V will provide shelf space in all locations for your cosmetics line."

Rae ran up behind me and hugged my neck. "Victoria are you serious?" "What kind of question is that woman? Of course I'm serious." I smiled for what seemed like the first time in hours.

"Congratulations babe!" Stephen kissed Rae and held up his glass.

"Okay one more toast. To Victor, thank you for not running out the door after we filled you in. To our favorite chef, Cher, thank you for making this phenomenal meal. To my dear Victoria and Sade, you know I will ride with you until the wheels fall off. Javier, my brother, you already know we are putting an end to the TJ madness. And to my warrior Rae, right now mama your job is to protect our legacy growing in your womb. I got the rest. Now let's eat."

This was one of Cher's many 'put you to sleep' right away dinners. We all look exhausted. I laid down on the couch next to Sade. I'm not sure when I fell asleep, but when I opened my eyes, I was in my new bed. I guess one of the guys carried me upstairs. When I turned over, my sweet Sade was right there next to me. Where else would she be? My big sister is always at my side when I need her. I am my sister's keeper. We need each other.

"Good morning Vic." "Good morning Sade. Yesterday really happened huh." "Yes Vic, unfortunately it wasn't a dream. Your family is here with you. TJ will be behind bars or dead, but he won't be harassing my little sister anymore."

Rae and Cher walked in and sat on the edge of the bed. Cher blew us both kisses before she started filling us in on the rest of the night.

"The guys put you and Sade to bed last night, and Rae and I came up shortly after. I think they were up most of the night strategizing and getting ready for today. Victor stayed with them. He just left to go home and freshen up. He'll be back to meet the security company when they arrive."

"Cher, did you say Victor stayed up all night with the guys?" "Yes ma'am Vic, that's exactly what I said."

Cher stood up and headed for the door. "Breakfast in twenty. Get up my sisters and get dressed. We need to focus on getting Vic ready for the grand opening. The guys are taking over the TJ situation for now."

Cher is in boss mode. When she can't deal with certain emotions, she turns into a drill sergeant. She means well, and I love her for it.

"Rae is with child now so we can't have her standing on her feet. I'll bring up a couple of the high back comfy bar stools from down stairs. It will be perfect for her to sit in front of us and do our makeup. But first ladies, please come with me to look through my gowns. You have to tell me which one I should wear to the grand opening."

"I'm going to lay down for a few minutes while you girls go pick out Cher's dress for the evening. Mommy and baby need a breather." Rae looks exhausted.

"Sounds great Rae, your body needs to rest. We will check on you soon. I guess we can move over to my wardrobe after Cher's and pick out my dress too. Rest well Rae. We love you." Sade leaned over and gave Rae a kiss on the forehead. Her tone was endearing. I know she misses my niece and nephew. Leo and Lea are her everything.

Six hours have passed and Rae hasn't risen. I peeped in on her an hour ago, and she was still knocked out.

All wardrobes are in check for the House of V grand opening. Never in my wildest dreams did I think I'd be opening a new store in Las Vegas.

I haven't talked to Cher about it yet, but I will be vacating the space on Fisher Island. The original location in Coral Gables will remain open, because Miami will always be home. I must admit, I am looking forward to life in Las Vegas for a while. Cher and I will talk after the grand opening. I know she will understand.

"Hey ladies, I'm going to run upstairs and check on Rae, why don't you two start your showers so by the time you're done Rae can start your makeup." "We're on it Vic. It's time to get glammed up, and forget about everything else for the next hours to come." Cher winked as she sauntered off with Sade in tow.

When I walked in the room Rae was already in the shower. She must have realized the time when she woke up, and decided to start getting ready for the evening. I'll run back downstairs and make her a cup of hot tea, and a small bowl of vanilla Greek yogurt topped with fruit and granola.

Rae shut the shower off as I walked back in the room. "Hey Rae it's me. I didn't want to startle you. I brought you a cup of hot tea and a little snack. How are you feeling?" "Thanks Vic. I'm okay. I think my body needed that rest though. This shower was the bomb too. I love how hot the water gets. It's a perfect massage for my back."

Rae cracked the bathroom door and looked out to see me standing in the doorway. We both smiled.

"Rae dearest, I hope you enjoy your tea and snack. I am going to jump in the shower now. Sade and Cher will be in first for makeup. They should be done with their showers now too." "Okay Auntie Vic."

With a mouth full, Rae smiled and her face lit up. She truly is glowing. I couldn't resist. I ran over to her, knelt down and kissed her gorgeous belly. I knew this little blessing deserved a strong mother and strong aunts. I stood up having it in my mind that I would follow Cher's suggestion. I will forget about everything, but the grand opening until it's over.

Within the next hour and a half Rae transformed our faces. I had everyone looking fabulous in their House of V designs. The look on their faces when they went to look at Cher's gown option was priceless. I had hung everyone's surprise in the room Cher is staying in. It's hilarious, they should know by now I always have a design or two up my sleeve for my sisters.

I am wearing a floor length, hot pink, off the shoulder gown with the tear drop diamond earrings momma gave to me for my birthday last year.

Cher's hour glass figure and olive complexion looks stunning in her black cocktail dress. Sade is wearing the hell out of the hot pink jumpsuit I made for myself. Paired with her Jimmy Choo heels, Sade is killing it. Once I was done making the jumpsuit, I knew it belonged in Sade's closet. Rae looks fabulous pregnant. Of course I had to pull together something special for my girl. She too is wearing black this evening. I made her a black jumpsuit that leaves plenty of breathing room for auntie's baby. Tonight is a big deal for both of us. I know Stephen and Javier are ready. We need to get a move on it.

"Looking stunning as always ladies." Javier spoke with a gleam in his eyes as he helped Sade down the last of the stairs.

We all thanked Javier, and Sade planted the sweetest kiss on his cheek. I'm so grateful to Javier for being here for us. Stephen spun Rae around slowly, taking in every inch of his woman's body.

"Alright, it's time to go. The limo is here." Stephen motioned for us to move towards the door. "We better get out of here while the getting is good. If we don't, I'm liable to rip this jumpsuit off of Rae, and well, you know the rest."

"We here you loud and clear Stephen. I agree, we need to head out. Mayor Howard is expected at seven sharp this evening for the ribbon cutting ceremony and photo opportunities. Her assistant just called to confirm that she will be on time. Mayor Howard always reminds her constituents that her time is precious, and she expects others to value their time just the same. We shall use our time wisely. Besides, we have a shit load of terror to deal with when we get back home tonight."

I am humbly grateful for my circle. I couldn't get through tonight without them. When we pulled up people were already enjoying the champaign, networking and having a great time. The jazz band was sending serene vibes through the crowd.

Victor walked up to us as we were approaching the door. He handed me a box. "Hello Victoria, you look lovely this evening. I bought you a little housewarming gift. Open it up."

What in the world. I started shaking the box from side to side. Victor pleaded, "Stop shaking it and just open the box woman."

I opened the box to find a really nice House of V black and gold plaque to hang on the wall just beside my front door. I love it.

"I love it Victor thank you so much." "You're welcome Vic, I'll come by to help you hang it up when you're ready. Now scoot up to the podium it's two minutes until seven and Mayor Howard just pulled up."

My girls followed me to the podium so that I could address everyone. Victor stayed behind to talk with Javier and Stephen. I imagine they are whispering about whatever plan they concocted to keep TJ away from us today. I do notice additional security personnel is present at the hotel today, specifically surrounding the House of V boutique. Victor said he would take care of it. It's comforting to know that he did. Mayor Howard also comes with her own security detail. In a flash, Mayor Howard was out of her vehicle and standing next to me at the podium.

After sharing my appreciation for my guests' presence at the grand opening, I surprised everyone by letting them know about the inclusion of Rae's cosmetics in our store locations. Rae provided each guest with a little treat in their gift bags and her company's contact information.

I then introduced Mayor Howard, whom everyone loves. She graciously welcomed House of V to the community, we cut the ribbon together and she was off. Of course, not before telling me she'd have her assistant call me to set up a lunch date. She would like to hire me to design her gown for the Governor's Black Tie Charity Gala. This year's gala will be held in the President's Ball Room at the Mediterranean Hotel. Located mid-strip, it is one of the nicest hotels built in Las Vegas within the last two years. It will be perfect for the ball. Wow, Mayor Howard asked me to design her gown. Las Vegas is shaping up to be a nice home away from home.

The grand opening went off without a hitch. I thank God for that. I hope TJ just crawls into a whole and disappears forever. Right on time, Sade is walking back up to me with a plate of sushi and a fresh glass of champaign. It's like she could feel the negative thoughts swimming to the surface or something.

"Sis I am so proud of you. I mean look at you Victoria. I know we have some crazy mess going on in our personal lives right now, but try to take in this moment. You've accomplished so much Victoria. You are truly living your professional dreams. You deserve to be proud of yourself. Allow yourself to be happy for a few uninterrupted moments little sis."

While Sade was talking Cher and Rae walked up behind us. We huddled into our usual circle, and as always I knew they had my back.

Chapter Nineteen

Dead or Alive

Sade

Thank goodness nothing happened last evening at Vic's grand opening. I will always blame myself for what my little sister felt she had to do to protect me. I'm the big sister. I first whispered, I am my sister's keeper in her ear when she was a baby. I always wanted to protect her from the world, and she is paying for doing just that for me. Years later the memories are forced back into the forefront. Back then, the only way I survived was by throwing myself into my studies and work. The unconditional love and support of my sister was and still is my foundation. TJ surfacing after all these years and reopening old wounds has my stomach in knots. I don't know how much more of this shit I can take.

What happened to the talks of wedding planning and honeymoon choices? I'm trying to sing from the mountaintop that I am happily engaged. Oh, or what about Rae and Stephen? Couldn't we have had five minutes to relish in the fact that they are expecting their first child? Shit, I already had to deal with biting my tongue over this Grace bullshit. Cher is my sister so of course I cut all professional and personal ties with Grace immediately. It was a mutual decision and a necessary action. It's crazy how you can know someone and really not know them at all. Hmm…that part. I didn't realize I was shaking my head until Rae started mocking my movements from across the room. So deep in thought, I didn't hear Rae come into the room.

"Good morning mama Rae." "Don't good morning mama Rae me woman. Spit it out. What are you over there so deep in thought about? And don't you dare say nothing cause I'm not hearing it."

"Rae, I'm just trying to figure out when we can have a break and feel free to celebrate the good without the evil constantly raining down on our parade. It breaks my heart seeing Vic suffer for being my hero again and again. I just want her to be able to focus on herself for a while. "I know you do Sade."

"Vic was there with me in the trenches throughout Joshua-Antonio and Annastasia nightmare. I don't know where I would be without my three sisters in my life. I need to end this for Vic. We need to be free to really move on."

Rae listened while I rambled on and on. She caught a break thanks to Javier calling out our names from downstairs.

"Sade. Cher. Rae. Vic. Get down here!" We all filed down the stairs. Stephen helped Rae get comfortable in my new oversized rocking chair. Javier continued, "Victor will be here in a few minutes. He has news about TJ."

"Victor has news?" "Yes Vic, he has news. Victor got a detective friend of his involved, and Stephen called in a few more favors from his FBI contact. We handled things on our own so you all could focus on the grand opening and each other."

Mr. Victor sure is being very helpful to my sister. Their friendship is new. I pray his intentions are good. I knew they were up to something. Javier and Stephen have been too calm the last twenty-four hours.

I leaned back between Rae's legs and glanced up at her. She placed her hand on my shoulder, and a sense of peace washed over me. Vic and Cher sat on the floor next to me. Hand in hand, we knew Victor was about to drop a bomb on us.

Stephen jumped up to open the door as soon as the chime started sounding. "Hey man we've all been sitting here going crazy waiting for you."

"Hey good people. I got here as fast as I could." "What's going on Victor?" "Good morning Victoria. Everyone."

Vic pleaded. "Talk to us, please." Victor walked over to Victoria and lifted her hands into his. He tightened his grip slightly. "TJ has been baker acted and he will be extradited back to Miami to face charges for Pierre's murder. He was arrested trying to break into the House of V. His ignorant, sick ass had the audacity to try to break into a boutique in a Las Vegas hotel. He was arrested about three o'clock this morning. His picture had already been circulated amongst our contacts. When he was arrested there was no question about his identity. They confiscated a gallon of gasoline from him. He was planning to burn the store and everything surrounding it to the ground."

Disbelief riddled our faces as Victor spoke. My mind wandered to the many late nights my little sis would put in at House of V Miami and Artistry. Tears began to stream down my face. Victoria could have been in her boutique working through the night. A psych ward isn't enough punishment. I am glad to see the agony ease in Vic's eyes, but it's not enough for me. I am my sister's keeper.

"What hospital was he taken too?" "Not that it matters Sade, but he's at Angel's Mercy. It's a mile from the precinct where he was booked before being baker acted." "It matters to me Victor."

Victoria walked over to the bar, poured a tall glass of whiskey and handed it to Victor. "I don't know how to thank you for helping us get rid of TJ. I'll never forget what you did for us." "You're welcome Victoria."

Cher made her way to the bar and poured five more glasses of whiskey and handed one to me, Javier, Stephen and Vic. I downed mine with one swallow. It's been a hell of a week. Javier held his glass up towards Victor to give a toast. "Welcome to the family man. You're stuck with us now." "Thanks Javier, stuck might not be so bad."

Victor looked down at Victoria and her cheeks flushed immediately. Victor is definitely interested in far more than a friendship with my sister.

"Thanks for looking out man. We barely know each other, but if you need anything don't hesitate to call. That's real Victor, don't hesitate." I hear you, and I thank you Stephen."

Javier wrapped his arms around me. I tried to steady my breathing. My head is swimming. "I want to go and lay down by the pool. I need a few moments alone honey." He leaned down and kissed me. "It's okay Sade, I understand."

"I'm not feeling too well myself. I think this little person growing inside of me is doing somersaults. I'm going to lay down next to Sade." Stephen rubbed Rae's back gently. The love in his eyes is heartwarming. "It's okay to rest Rae. We aren't going anywhere." "I love you Stephen." " love you too Rae."

Rae followed me outside with both hands resting on her stomach. I caught her giving me the side eye. I swear that woman can read me like a book. Before I could sit down she lit into me.

"I know damn well your ass isn't tired. What the hell are you scheming up in your head?" "Look Rae, if you're not with me, then I'm not talking."

"Since when am I not with you Sade. We ride together for life. You know this sis. Now talk to me."

"Rae, I want him dead. I don't want to spend the rest of my days wondering if he will escape from prison or the psych ward. I worry about Victoria and her safety. I feel so much guilt for what she's been through to protect me. And, I am terrified for the lives of my children. I buried my memories of Theodore for so long. Knowing that TJ was just standing there watching me suffer is killing me inside. As long as he breathes, I will fear for my sister's safety."

Rae searched my face trying to find the right words to comfort me. Without saying anything, she grabbed my hand, and told me to follow her. We walked around the side of the house to the front. She bent down near the driver side tire of Stephen's rental truck. He rented a black Ford F150 the following morning we arrived. I heard the car door unlock. Rae motioned for me to get in.

"Where are we going Rae?" "Just get in Sade, you'll see when we get there." "Seriously Rae, where are we going woman. I feel a migraine coming on, and I'm too emotional to play games right now." "Sade no one is playing games."

Rae leaned over and opened the glove compartment. "Betty? What is Stephen doing with Betty in the truck." "Stephen didn't put it there, I did sis. Pregnancy hasn't altered my aim. That's one thing I can hold on to from Matthew and our lessons. That damn Matthew. That's a whole other crisis we have to deal with. I'll never understand how he fucked up with Cher."

What seemed like five minutes later, Rae was pulling into the guest parking lot at Angel's Mercy Hospital. "Alright Sade, I know it's underhanded, but I looked through Victor's cell phone. I saw a text message from the detective. I know what room TJ is being held in."

"So what do you think we are about to do Rae? Waltz up in here and fire a gun off in the hospital?" "No, the gun is just there in case we need it when we leave the hospital. You know I'm a chemist first and foremost."

Rae opened up the center console, unzipped her small makeup case and pulled a syringe and small medication vial out. Right then I knew this would be the last day I ever have to deal with TJ. I stopped asking questions. Our eyes locked for a few minutes.

"You good Rae. My little baby cakes that you're carrying comes first always." "Yes Sade, we are both good."

Rae leaned in the back seat and pulled out her volunteer work bag. She volunteers in the Chemistry department at Redding University in Doral once a week. She threw me one of her lab coats. We put the coats on. Instantly it masked her pregnancy, and we will blend in with the staff.

Without much thought, our plan that wasn't a plan was coming together. Rae can't take the hit for this though. While I am grateful that she has the means, I prefer to handle this myself. It's too personal for me.

TJ sat there just watching his father ram into me over and over again while slamming my head against the wall. I wonder what TJ would have done if Victoria hadn't walked in. I wonder if he knew that wasn't the first time, just the last?

I hate TJ for relishing in my embarrassing and brutally violating misery. I usually don't let that thought surface. It wasn't the first time the night Vic saved me. I just refused to acknowledge or discuss more than I had to. That was my personal secret from hell.

I voiced aloud that I thought Ashton was killed by his coach, or someone that was upset about him not following the exact sports path they laid out for him. Deep down in my soul, I have always believed it possible too that Theodore could have killed him. He saw me running off to college with Ashton as my way to escape his wrath. Theodore knew I wouldn't tell my family about what he had done to me two times prior to the night he was caught and killed. Now I get to look TJ in the face and see his response when I ask him if his father killed Ashton. I never threw it out there, because I didn't want the authorities to connect Vic to Theodore's murder.

"Snap out of it. Are you ready Sade. Baker acted patients are held on the second floor until moved to their outpatient location." "My thoughts are just running a mile a minute Rae, but I have never been more ready."

When Rae wasn't paying attention I slipped the syringe and vial in my inside lab coat pocket.

"Rae, when we get to the room, I would like to speak with him alone first. There's a few thoughts I need to get off my chest privately, please." "Yes Vic, I get it." "I love you Rae."

We made our way to the second floor unnoticed. Rae had an extra badge so we clipped them onto our lab coats, and conveniently turned the wording facing our chest. We would have known which room was TJ's immediately, because his room is the only one with a guard placed right out front. We went to the restroom on the floor for a few minutes to by some time. I told Rae to wait inside the restroom for me to come back. I went back down the hall, and peeped my head around the corner. The guard was gone so I started for TJ's room door. Once inside TJ's room my adrenaline shot through the roof.

TJ's eyes are open, yet it seems like he's sleeping. "TJ." "Sade, is that you?" "Yes asshole, it's me." "What the hell are you doing here. How did you get in my hospital room? Where is the guard?"

"I'll be asking the questions TJ." "What questions?"

"First of all, I just have to know if the night your father was killed was the first night you knew he had been raping me?" "Why does that matter now Sade?" I looked at TJ in disgust. He turned his head toward the window as if to ignore my presence.

"That's answer enough for me. You knew, you watched and you enjoyed seeing me suffer." "It was better you than me. You became his new distraction after years of torturing me for my mother's indiscretions. Theodore couldn't handle finding out that my mother had a child with another man. I watched him stand over her as she had what would be her final seizure, and do nothing to help her. He waited for her body to become still, and her last breath to be taken. Finding out I was not his son broke him. I was a constant reminder of his hatred for my mother. You gave me a reprieve, however sickening it was."

Theodore looked at me as if he expected me to sympathize. I care not! "If that is true TJ, then I will never understand why you weren't happy about Theodore's death?" "I don't understand it either, but I hold a sick sense of loyalty to him. "I had no one, only Theodore. Victoria took him from me."

Listening to TJ try to explain his thought process is making me nauseous. I am nervous to hear the answer to my next question.

"I have one more question TJ." "What is it?" "Did Theodore kill Ashton too?" TJ laughed. His laughter made my body cringe.

"No you naïve bitch, I did. I couldn't have that little pro athlete want to whisk you away from Theodore. He was just in the way. Besides who the hell said he gets to live the good life while I'm over here fighting for mine. So I offed his ass too. I knew my father had his sights on you far before he ever made his first move. Till this day I can't believe your dad never suspected anything. My father was a heathen through and through, yet ninety-nine percent of the people he interacted with would never know it."

I was in shock. TJ just admitted to killing Ashton too. I pulled the vial out of my coat pocket, and rammed it into TJ's intravenous tube. I ran out of the room and didn't look back. I turned the corner as fast as I could and flung the bathroom door open.

"It's about time Sade. I didn't think you'd be in there that long." "I know Rae." "Alright let's get back in the room so I can do what I do."

Rae felt in her pocket for the vial and syringe. "Oh shit, I must have dropped it in the car." "Maybe that's a sign Rae. I asked my questions. Let's just go."

We rode the elevator in silence. When the elevator doors opened, we speed walked to the exit. By the time we made it to the valet awning, they were calling a code blue over the intercom, but we were unable to make out the room number. I'd rather Rae think that I just changed my mind. Thinking that she dropped the vial and syringe is easier for me. Rae was breathing a little heavy by the time we made it to the car. I had a water bottle in my hand when we left the house. I pulled it out of the cup holder and opened it up for Rae.

"Here, take a couple sips before you pull off." Rae finished the bottle in a few gulps. We stopped at the liquor store to pick up a few bottles of wine. That would be our excuse for leaving if anyone happened to notice we were gone.

When we pulled into the driveway at the house my heart sank beneath the soles of my feet. It's finally over. Now I just have to act like I don't know it's over. I stuffed the lab coats back in

Rae's volunteer work bag while she looked for the vial and syringe.

"Where the hell could I have dropped it." "Rae, I looked under the seats, I don't see it. I think we should get back inside before the calvary has a million and one questions." "You're right sis, it's been a hell of a wine run Sade."

I grabbed the wine bag and we walked back around the house the same way we left. I placed the wine in the wine cooler behind the pool bar. Rae lay back on the pool chair, and I poured her a glass of iced tea.

"Have a cold glass of tea Rae. Give my baby a little sugary goodness. It seems like no one noticed we were even gone." "Sade, take your ass over to the bar, pour a large glass of wine and come sit next to me." I followed Rae's orders and took a nice sip on my way back.

"Here's to us having each other's back no matter what. I am my sister's keeper Sade. You, Vic and Cher are my sisters for life. Period." "Thank you always Rae, we love you too!"

Victoria came running outside. Cher and Javier were right behind her.

"Victor just woke me up from my nap. His detective friend called him to let him know that TJ had been pronounced dead less than an hour ago.

He didn't have any details about the cause of death. He only confirmed that TJ is dead. Victor said he'll be coming back over soon."

Everyone had an awkward sense of relief blanketing their face except for me and my Rae of sun. Rae looked at me, and I looked down at my glass of wine. No words were necessary. She knows exactly what happened to her vial and syringe now.

The End

CONNECT with Author, *Kilene 'Ki' Williams*
sales@oceanviewpromotions.com
Www.OceanViewPromotions.com

PLEASE rate and leave a review. It's one of the best ways to support independent authors.